WITCH'S CAULDRON

LEGION OF ANGELS: BOOK 2

ELLA SUMMERS

WITCH'S CAULDRON
Legion of Angels: Book 2

www.ellasummers.com/witchs-cauldron

ISBN 978-1-5410-0915-8

BOOKS BY ELLA SUMMERS

Legion of Angels

Vampire's Kiss

Witch's Cauldron

Siren's Song

Dragon's Storm

Shifter's Shadow

Psychic's Spell

Fairy's Touch

Angel's Flight

Dragon Born Serafina

Mercenary Magic

Magic Games

Magic Nights

Rival Magic

Dragon Born Shadow World

(Magic Eclipse, Midnight Magic, Magic Storm)

The Complete Trilogy

Dragon Born Alexandria

Magic Edge

Blood Magic

Magic Kingdom

Dragon Born Awakening

Fairy Magic

Spirit Magic

Magic Immortal

And more books coming soon…

WITCH'S CAULDRON

Something wicked is brewing in New York.

"A month ago, I watched in horror as six of my fellow initiates died after sipping the Nectar of the gods, a heavenly drink that either grants you magical powers or kills you. I can't believe I'm coming back for seconds."

Leda Pierce has survived the gods' first test and gained entry into the Legion of Angels, but the fight is far from over. Someone is poisoning the supernaturals of New York. Suspecting witches, the Legion sends in Leda to investigate. To save the city, she will need magic she doesn't have—and gaining that magic might just kill her. Now her survival depends on accepting help from the darkly seductive angel Nero, but that help comes with a price she cannot afford to pay.

Witch's Cauldron is the second book in the *Legion of Angels* series.

CHAPTERS

CHAPTER TWENTY-FOUR

Life and Death / 223

CHAPTER 1

DO OR DIE

*A*n angel stood behind me, his arms locked across mine in an iron grip. I pulled and pushed and heaved, but he didn't budge an inch. Angels were stubborn like that.

"I have you right where I want you," I told him, yanking on his arms.

"And where is that?" Nero didn't move. He was like a mountain—a mountain of muscle and infuriating willpower.

I looked up at the high ceiling of the gym, searching for insight that didn't come. I had no idea how I was going to get out of this situation, but I wasn't about to tell him that. Fake it until you make it.

"Give me a moment, and you'll see," I declared.

I continued to push against his hold. I had the strength of a vampire, but while that gave me the edge I needed against humans, it was wholly useless against angels. They had the strength of vampires too—and then some.

"I'm waiting," he said, a hint of amusement breaking through the hard shell of his words.

"Almost there," I puffed out. "And it's going to be epic."

"Take your time," he chuckled.

Apparently, my useless attempts to free myself were enormously funny. I tried to shift my weight to slide my arms out of his grip, but he wasn't having any of that. No matter what I did, his hold didn't relax, not even for a second. As I slammed my back into him, I became acutely aware of the hard contours of his chest. My eyes dipped to his arms, thick and tight around me. I was hit with the sudden urge to see the rest of him—to touch and taste the rest of him. I shoved that thought right out of my head. There would be no touching and absolutely no tasting.

I had an unhealthy addiction to Nero's blood. It was like a drug, a drug I couldn't get enough of. Even now, I could feel his pulse popping against my skin, tempting me. I blamed the vampire magic the Legion of Angels had given me. I wasn't a vampire per se, but I did have their abilities and their hunger. If I lived long enough, I'd receive the magic of a whole bunch of other supernaturals too.

"You might want to rethink your strategy, Leda," Nero said, his breath hot on my neck.

Gods, he was making it hard to concentrate. Not that he was *doing* anything—well, besides standing there, slowly squeezing the air out of my lungs. His scent flooded me, the scent of angel and sex. I shook my head. Whoa, where had that come from? It must be the delirium setting in as my body screamed for oxygen. I had to get free.

I tried to push back, to slam him against the wall. His feet remained planted to the ground. He was too strong. I kicked back at his shins, but he blocked me with his feet. How could he even move that fast?

"You aren't making this easy," I growled, stomping down on his foot. At least I tried to. He moved his foot aside, and my heel thumped against the gym floor.

"That's the point."

I threw back my head, slamming it into his face. He still didn't budge, even though that must have hurt like hell. Well, it had hurt *me*. Spots danced in front of my eyes, rapid and blinking. Breathing was getting difficult.

The next thing I knew, I was facing Nero, his hands locked on my arms, holding me up. I blinked back blackness, trying to focus. I'd passed out. Again. That was the third time today, and it wasn't even dawn yet.

Nero stepped back. "Again."

I groaned. Just the thought of fighting him again made every bone in my body scream in protest.

"That is not an attitude befitting a soldier of the Legion," he lectured me. "We must be strong, dignified, unerring."

"It's hard to be any of those things at five o'clock in the morning."

"So you wish to stop our training sessions?"

"No." I shook out my arms and legs. "I can do this."

Nero had been working with me every morning before everyone else got up for normal training. He was helping me get strong, and I *did* appreciate it—ok, maybe not so much when I was stuck in the middle of that help, which often felt more like torture.

A busy angel like Nero had better things to do than babysit a first level soldier like me. And yet here he was, waking up early too when he could have just slept in. Instead he was spending this time with me, training me. I didn't want to disappoint him. And more than that, I couldn't afford to give up. Getting knocked around the room a few times was nothing compared to what lay before me. I needed to be ready.

He motioned me forward, and I began walking toward him.

"Stop," he said.

I froze. "What?"

"What have you learned?"

"To follow your orders." I'd tried to maintain a perfectly serious face, but mischief must have sparkled in my eyes because he sighed.

He stepped around me, locking me in that unbreakable hold again. "Your opponent has you trapped like this. What do you do?" he asked me.

"Stomp on your feet. Kick your shins," I said immediately. "But you are too fast."

"What else?"

"Slam my head back into your face." For all the good it had done me last time. Nero was too stubborn to flinch. If anything, he'd held on even more tightly. "None of that works on *you*, though. You're too big. Too strong. Too heavy."

"Use that against me," he said, each word vibrating with delicious warmth as it fell on my throat.

My pulse popped hard against my skin, the blood rushing like a burning river, searing my veins, begging him to bite me. I thought back to the last time he'd bitten me. The memory shot a ruthless, primal desire through me, stripping away all propriety and reason. The rational part of my brain was hanging on by a thin strand.

But I had to hold on. I cleared my throat and said, "How do I use your strength against you?" My voice creaked as pitifully as my sore bones.

"Lean over," Nero said, hardly above a whisper.

He pressed his body harder against mine, the pressure making me bend at the waist—and think really indecent thoughts.

"Use my own weight to throw me." He straightened, but

the pressure remained. He'd committed most of his weight forward. "Now."

I moved quickly, using his weight to pull him over my shoulder—and sure enough, I was able to throw him. My victory was short-lived, however. Even as he fell, he didn't let go of my arms, and so I fell too, landing on him. Before I could move, he flipped us over so that he was on top of me. I tried to struggle free, but of course I couldn't. The damn angel had pinned me to the floor. I glared up at him.

"Glaring is not an effective attack," he said smugly.

I imagined his head exploding. I broadcast that picture to him, loud and clear. He had telepathic magic, so he might just pick it up.

His mouth curled into a smile. "Yes, that attack would work better. *If* you had such an ability. As it is, you'll just have to make do with what you do have."

"What's the point of telling me how to get out of your hold if I can't actually get out of your hold?" I demanded.

Nero rolled back, sliding up to his feet. "Because it will work on most of the opponents you face. Even if it doesn't work on me." He extended his hand down to me, pulling me up.

"You're really arrogant, you know."

"I'm an angel."

"Yeah, I know. Arrogance comes with the wings."

"This isn't about arrogance. Angels are faster and more resilient than other people. As you well know."

Yeah, I did know. I had learned a lot from Nero—and used it on my opponents in training. Like he said, the things he taught me were effective against most people. In fact, they worked really well.

"You could let me win once in a while," I said.

"And what purpose would that serve?"

"It would make me feel better."

"It would make you feel better to know that I let you win?" His eyebrows crept up.

"Yes," I said stubbornly.

"That's not how we do things here."

I sighed. "I know."

The Legion of Angels was a do-or-die kind of place. Our magic was gifted to us by the gods, a new power every time we advanced up the ranks. It was kind of like a really twisted real-life video game. With each new level, Legion soldiers received the powers of a different supernatural, boosts like the physical abilities of vampires, the potion-brewing power of witches, and the healing magic of fairies.

The catch—and oh, yes, there was a big one—was if your will wasn't strong enough to absorb the gift, it killed you outright. Just two months ago, I'd watched over twenty people die during my initiation ceremony into the Legion. Even more of my fellow initiates had died when we'd all drunk from the Nectar of the gods to receive our first gift, Vampire's Kiss.

The Legion took all kinds of people—those who wanted to prove themselves, those who craved power, and those who were simply desperate. I was of the glorious latter category. I'd joined the Legion to gain telepathic magic, a skill called Ghost's Whisper. It would give me the ability to link into the minds of my loved ones, and that power was my only chance of finding my kidnapped brother.

The only problem was Ghost's Whisper was a level nine ability in the Legion. In order to gain it, I'd have to survive all the trials before it. That included getting my wings and becoming an angel. It was called the Legion of Angels because the angels commanded the gods' army, but there weren't many angels in the world. Very few made it that far up the Legion. But I *had* to. My brother was counting on me to beat the odds, and if there was one thing I excelled at, it was my unwavering stubbornness. So I stared that angel down and resolved to kick his ass.

Nero nodded in approval. "We'll go again."

I began to circle around him. "Will I ever be able to defeat you?"

"After you've gained more powers."

"And before that?"

His face was unreadable, as cold as marble. "Perhaps."

"How?"

"You have to find my weaknesses and exploit them."

"Care to share?"

He remained silent.

"Yeah, I didn't think so."

He wasn't going to hand me anything. He was going to make me fight for it. I swung a punch at him, but he caught my fist, holding me back.

"You know, you are really aggravating," I told him.

He said nothing, but I thought I caught a hint of amusement on his face—just a second before his grip tightened and he flipped me down to the floor. I rolled, jumping up.

"I need a weapon," I commented.

"The rules of this match are quite clear. No weapons."

"Yeah, I know. You love your rules."

Sometimes we fought with no weapons. Sometimes we fought with just one particular weapon. Nero defined the rules of each match very clearly. He wanted to make sure I was a master of any weapon—and that I stopped using found objects to fight. I wasn't allowed to knock my opponent upside the head with a trashcan lid, even if that lid was lying right there just begging to be used. Apparently, such tactics weren't very dignified. And soldiers of the Legion were *always* dignified.

"How about I get a weapon and you don't?" I suggested, smirking at him.

"There is little value in teaching you to fight only in situations where you are at an advantage over your opponent."

"Instead I should always be at a disadvantage," I muttered.

"Besides," he continued, as though I hadn't said a thing. "I don't think giving you a weapon would be the advantage you think it is."

"Because you would just steal it and use it against me," I realized.

He nodded.

"And you claim you are civilized. You're just as dirty as I am."

His eyebrows arched.

"You know what I mean," I said, flushing.

He swung at me. I ducked, avoiding his fist. Ha! I wasn't as strong as Nero, but I was quick. Just not quick enough. Moving so fast that his hand was a blur, he followed up with a punch that knocked me to the floor.

"Get up," he said over my aching body.

Rather than get up, though, I just lay there this time, pretending to be unconscious. Nero might have been a hard ass, but he was helping me. He was training me and not because he liked hurting me. He knew about my brother, knew that he was a telepath, but he was keeping it from the gods, who would try to find Zane themselves and force him into their service. Nero was doing all of this for me. Maybe *I* was his weakness.

So I waited until he bent down to check on me, then I quickly kicked out, knocking him down. As soon as he hit the floor, I jumped on top of him, pinning him down. I opened my mouth to laugh out in victory, but the angel knocked me off of him with a blast of telekinetic magic.

"Hey!" I shouted, scrambling to my feet. "No magic. That's not fair."

"Since when has war ever been fair?"

"So I have to play by your rules, but you don't?"

"Yes."

I glowered at him.

"And pretending to be unconscious was not befitting of a soldier of the Legion," he said.

"But it wasn't against your rules."

"It was implied."

He was so close now, almost within striking distance. Before I could contemplate the recklessness of what I was about to do, I surged forward, straight at him. My impulsiveness paid off. I landed a blow to his stomach. Nero's eyes flashed in surprise, but he quickly recovered. I didn't get in another hit. He grabbed me and slammed me to the ground. My back hit the floor with the resounding thump of defeat, and he pinned me down for the fifty-third time today.

"I hate you," I growled up at him.

"I warned you that you would hate me before this was over."

"I will get back at you," I promised.

He stared down at me with perfect calmness. "And how are you going to do that?"

By sabotaging the hot water on the twenty-third floor so you get only ice water when you turn on your shower. Or by sneaking into your apartment and spreading superglue all across the insides of your clothes.

"I would have to punish your transgression," he warned me.

9

I clenched my jaw. "Get out of my head."

Usually, I could keep him out so that he only saw what I chose to broadcast to him.

"Your emotions are running hot right now. Your thoughts are so vivid that it's hard to ignore them," he said, his hands tightening around mine.

I trailed my gaze up the hard, merciless muscles in his arms, all the way up to his chest, which was taut beneath the thin fabric of his shirt. It was a good thing my hands were pinned over my head because I would have had a hard time resisting the urge to scrape my fingernails across his chest and down his back.

"That would be inappropriate," he told me. And yet he leaned in, inhaling deeply, as though he were drinking in my scent.

There were a lot of things an angel with his heightened senses could tell from my scent, things I didn't want him knowing any more than I wanted him inside of my head. I swallowed hard, trying to shield my mind and calm my racing pulse. I didn't care much if he caught me fantasizing about playing pranks on him, but I didn't want him to see me fantasizing about less innocuous things. Naked things.

A sexy smile twisted Nero's lips. Shit. He'd heard that too. But he didn't say a thing. He just stared down at me, his mouth dangerously close to mine, his chest brushing against me each time he breathed.

The door to the gym hall closed loudly. I turned my head and looked at the woman who'd just entered. Dressed in a black leather Legion uniform that was as black as her chin-length hair, she was gorgeous. Between her dark hair and pale skin, she looked like Snow White—well, if Snow White were a soldier of the Legion rather than a fictitious fairytale princess.

"Colonel Windstriker," she said, her words pulsing with strength beneath the melodic lilt of her voice. "Am I interrupting something?" Her blue eyes darted to me.

"No." Nero rose quickly, hurrying toward her. Then he dropped to his knees before her. "My apologies, First Angel."

So this beautiful stranger was an angel. No, not just an angel—the top angel of the Legion, the leader of the gods' army. What was she doing here?

The First Angel lifted her hands. "Rise."

Nero did as she'd asked, but he didn't say anything. He simply looked at her, waiting for her to speak again.

Her gaze flickered to me once more before settling on him. "Come with me, Colonel. We have much to discuss."

He walked with her across the gym hall, stopping at the door to call back to me, "Get moving. Captain Somerset is expecting you in Hall Four in half an hour."

Then he turned and followed the First Angel out of the room.

CHAPTER 2

INFINITE IMPOSSIBILITIES

*A*fter Nero and the First Angel left the gym hall, I hurried down the corridor to Demeter, the Legion's canteen. I grabbed a quick breakfast of scrambled eggs, toast, and orange juice, then joined my friends Ivy and Drake at our usual table. They looked fresh and awake this morning; they must have gotten to the coffee before it had run out. It *always* ran out before I got here. Every single morning. The cynic in me was convinced Nero purposely kept me in training until the morning coffee was gone. The angel believed any weakness—even a minor one like caffeine dependence—was a mortal failing in a soldier of the Legion. I'd noticed it *had* been getting easier to wake up since I'd ditched the morning coffee, but I wasn't about to tell him that. I wasn't even going to think it in case he managed to tune in to my thoughts again.

"I saved a donut for you," Ivy said, her long, red hair bouncing off her shoulders as she turned her head to look up at me.

"Thanks," I replied, sitting down opposite her and Drake.

Ivy had the body of a supermodel, but she'd put on

more muscle in the past two months. Drake had the wide shoulders and build of a football player—which he'd been before joining the Legion. But his smile was so good-natured, so friendly. If I hadn't seen him tear werewolves apart with his bare hands, I'd have had a hard time believing he could ever get angry. But as soon as Ivy had been in danger, he'd broken through those werewolves, no fear in him, only rage—like a switch had been flipped inside of his brain.

The two of them looked so beautiful together, even though they weren't actually *together*. They were both wearing the standard Legion workout suits just like I was. But they hadn't been training since five in the morning, so their clothes were unwrinkled and clean. And they didn't smell like sweat and angel.

Ivy's gaze panned down my body. "Early morning?" she asked, a smile spreading her mouth.

"Too early. Like every morning." I took a bite out of the donut. A jolt of energy shook my body. Whoa. "Did I mention I'm not a morning person?"

Drake laughed. "Only every single morning."

I sighed, finishing up the donut. Whatever magic was in it, I wanted more. "What I wouldn't give for a long bath."

I shared a dorm room with five people. We had one shower. And no bathtub.

I rolled back my neck, stretching out the stiffness in it. "A long bath and a massage." I sighed.

Ivy smirked at me. "Why don't you ask Colonel Sexy Pants for a massage?" That was her name for Nero. "I bet he'd oblige," she added with a mischievous twinkle in her brown eyes.

I poked the eggs on my plate. "He was too busy throwing me across the gym to listen to requests for a massage."

"You two sure have been spending a lot of time together," she said. "People are talking. Especially the brats."

The Legion brats were people with an angel parent, and there were six of them in our initiation class. Their bloodline ensured they had more magic in them than most people, and they'd been trained from birth to join the Legion like their parents before them. They also had the egos to go with their esteemed pedigree.

"What do the brats say?" I asked.

"That you're failing combat training and had to take remedial classes," Drake said.

"But they're just jealous they don't have a sexy angel training them one-on-one," Ivy added quickly.

"Training with an angel is not all it's cracked up to be, you know," I told them. "I wasn't kidding about that bath and massage. I feel like my body has been put through a meat grinder."

"Didn't he heal you?" Ivy asked.

"No, he got distracted."

She wiggled her eyebrows at me. "I'll bet."

"No, not like *that*. The First Angel walked into our training session." I spread raspberry marmalade across my toast. "I wonder what she's doing here."

"She's here to investigate the supernaturals in New York in the aftermath of what happened last month," said Ivy. "Her team is rounding up vampires, witches, and shifters all over the city and interrogating them, trying to figure out how much of a foothold into this world the demons have gotten. They believe the demons are still recruiting for their army."

"How can you possibly know about this?"

"I chatted with Captain Horn and Lieutenant Bradshaw on the way to breakfast this morning, and they told me," she said, as though it were perfectly normal for two officers of the

Legion to openly share information like that. Then again, people were always telling Ivy things. It was astounding how much she could get out of someone just by smiling at them. "The First Angel thinks the demons' influence on Earth is stronger than we thought. And she believes that even though the Legion took out the operation at Sweet Dreams, this is far from over."

Ivy's smile faded during that last sentence. Her mother had been the one behind recruiting people for the demons' army, the act of a desperate woman dying of cancer. In exchange for the demons making her immortal, she'd made a deal with them to set up this operation. She hadn't told Ivy about any of this. Ivy had found out the hard way. After the battle at the Sweet Dreams bakery, I'd had to be the one to tell my friend that her mother was dead.

A month later, Ivy was still struggling with her conflicting feelings. On the one hand, Rose had been the head of recruitment for a demon army. On the other hand, she was Ivy's mother. Ivy loved her mother but hated what she'd done. The whole thing was tearing her up inside.

I reached across the table and gave Ivy's hand a good squeeze. She squeezed me back, wiping her tears away and putting on a happy face. She wasn't the best fighter in our group, but she was more resilient than people gave her credit for.

———

AFTER BREAKFAST, WE HEADED OVER TO HALL FOUR, where Captain Somerset was waiting for us. Nero had overseen our initial training, but as the top ranking person in New York—and the only angel—he had more important things to do than to spend his days torturing lowly soldiers.

That was now Captain Somerset's job, and she took that job very seriously.

We approached cautiously to see what the good captain had for us today. Yesterday it had been a field trip to the plains of monsters to go hunting for a pack of fire wolves. As someone who'd grown up next door to the plains of monsters, I'd learned that you never crossed that big stone and magic wall standing between us and the beasts who'd taken over half of the Earth. Sure I'd ignored that sensible rule a few times in my years as a bounty hunter, but I'd never gone hunting for monsters out there. It was insane. When I'd told Captain Somerset that, she'd responded that the Legion didn't require sanity from its soldiers, only obedience. She'd almost managed to keep a straight face as she'd said it.

Today's offering wasn't monsters or field trips beyond the wall. Instead, Captain Somerset had set up the gym hall with an obstacle course of infinite impossibilities.

"Come in closer now. Don't be shy," she said, grinning. She might have been trying to kill us, but at least she was doing it with a smile.

"What is that?" Toren said, his eyes widening as he looked up at the obstacle course looming over us like a storm cloud ready to let loose.

"That is your latest challenge," Captain Somerset declared.

"That's not challenging. It's impossible," Lucy gasped.

"Some of those jumps just aren't even doable," Lyle agreed.

"You have supernatural skills," the captain reminded us. "You have the speed, strength, and stamina of vampires."

"And the self-healing too," said Roden, one of the brats. "If we fall and get hurt, we can just nibble a little on Ivy's neck to heal ourselves." He flashed her a grin, and the other brats chuckled.

Ivy smiled at them. "Sorry, not my type." Everyone knew Ivy had a thing for the Legion officers—and that they had a thing for her.

"Ok, enough chitchat. Shut up and listen," Captain Somerset told us.

Had Nero been here, he would have made us run laps or do pushups for talking. He believed if you had enough energy to talk, you weren't pushing yourself hard enough— and so *he* pushed you harder. But Nero wasn't here, and I really needed to stop thinking about him. Obsessing over an angel wasn't healthy. I had to get a new hobby. Like eating chocolate. There wasn't anything unhealthy about that.

"You will begin the course with a dash across these raised platforms," Captain Somerset said. "But beware. If you put your weight on any one of them for too long, it will drop to the floor. The final platform in the sequence leads to a big jump directly onto this climbing wall." She indicated a leap worthy of a spider. "The climb will bring you to your next challenge."

She walked beneath a series of wooden posts twenty feet up. Hall Four had the highest ceiling of any of the Legion's gyms. Maybe this was where they taught angels how to fly. No, come to think of it, they probably just pushed new angels off the roof of the building. That was more like the Legion's style.

"Jump from one post to the next until you reach the tightrope," she said. "After a quick walk across the rope, a jump into this vertical tunnel awaits you. Next is a dash through a labyrinth. Some of the walls are equipped with motion sensors and will shoot out smoke and debris at you as you pass."

Someone coughed in disbelief behind me, but I wasn't surprised. For the past two months, the Legion had been putting us into one difficult situation after the other—and they'd made no secret of the fact that they didn't expect all of us to survive. From the fifty people who'd shown up at the initiation ceremony, only sixteen of us remained.

"After you escape the labyrinth of exploding walls, a door stands in your way."

She led us to a metal door we all knew well. It was identical to the ones Nero had put us in front of every day for weeks. He'd made us punch the door again and again until our hands bled, and we'd learned to tune out that pain. He'd called it an exercise in willpower, and it really was. It had taken enormous willpower not to punch him instead. As it was, I'd just imagined his face on the door while punching it.

But I wasn't supposed to be thinking about Nero. I returned my full attention to Captain Somerset.

"Each time you punch the door, it will open a little more, until the opening is wide enough for you to go through," she explained, passing the door. "On the other side, your final challenge awaits."

She indicated a bar used for pull-ups—except these weren't mere pull-ups in store for us. To complete this challenge, we had to hop the bar up a series of levels until we reached the top. And then we had to hop the bar back down again, level by level. The best part was we had to do all of this while our hands were still bleeding from punching that door how many ever times it took to open it.

"After you're finished with the salmon ladder, hop down onto the landing platform. Then run ten laps on the track before you get in line for the course again," Captain Somerset finished.

She put half of us in line in front of the obstacle course

and assigned the other half to run laps as they waited. I was third in line. I watched two others struggle through the obstacles before me. We were all still working on mastering our vampire abilities—some of us more than others. After all, it hadn't been so many weeks ago that we'd received the gods' first gift. When the Legion didn't have a job for us, we trained the whole day long. Lots and lots of training. The key to surviving the gods' gifts of magic was willpower, so every training session we did was designed to force our bodies and minds to the breaking point.

I pushed through the course, refusing to give up even as it tested my muscles in new and excruciating ways. I had to make it through, to make my body accept all the magic I'd been given. It was not automatic. You had to master one gift before you got the next. That was how the Legion of Angels worked—and I had eight more levels to go before I could gain the power I needed to find my brother.

I'd made it past the insanity of the exploding walls and was halfway through the final challenge when Nero stepped into the gym hall. He looked fresh out of the shower, every drop of water visible on his mostly dry hair. I watched him walk across the room to Captain Somerset, and my distracted mind cost me. My hands slipped, and I nearly fell off my bar. I could have sworn I caught a hint of amusement on his lips before it was swallowed by his usual marble expression.

Cursing that arrogant angel, I powered through the rest of the course, then hopped down. I closed up beside Ivy on the track, and we ran our ten laps together. As we entered the line for round two, Drake was just entering the obstacle course. Ivy's eyes were glued to him, so of course I had to tease her about it.

"Enjoying the show?" I asked her, keeping my voice low

so Nero didn't hear me. If he realized I was chatting, he'd assign me more laps.

"Are you?" Ivy shot back with a grin, her eyes darting between me and Nero.

His stare honed in on us, as though he'd heard us. He opened his mouth, but his phone rang at that moment, saving the day.

"Not that I blame you," Ivy added, sighing. "That angel looks good enough to eat."

"Nah, I'd choke on all the feathers."

The corner of Ivy's mouth drew up into a smirk. "He's really helped you, Leda. You're getting faster and stronger every day."

"Tell that to my ribs," I said, pulling up my shirt to show her the bruised skin on my side.

"Those are impressive love marks, honey."

"You can see the imprint of his fist. I'd hardly call that a love mark."

Ivy shrugged. "He's an angel."

It was her turn to take on the obstacle course, so she hurried forward.

"No, I'll handle this myself," Nero said into his phone, walking toward me. He slid the phone into his jacket. "Pandora," he said, using his nickname for me. "Fireswift, Ravenfall." He motioned to Jace and Mira, two of the Legion brats. Apparently, there was some unspoken Legion rule that stated the children of angels got to be called by their parents' esteemed surnames—those magical names bestowed upon Legion soldiers when they became angels—rather than being stuck with mocking nicknames like the rest of us. "Come with me."

We followed Nero out of the gym hall, leaving the others to deal with Captain Somerset's obstacle course. Hellish as it was, I had a feeling it was harmless compared to whatever Nero was about to have us do. He didn't leave the office to rescue cats from trees or to parade down the street for the delight of the city's residents.

"There's been an attack on the city," Nero said, not slowing for a second as he led us down the corridor toward the Legion's garage.

"What kind of attack?" I asked.

"Every single person in a ten-story building suddenly dropped dead."

CHAPTER 3

THE NEW YORK MASSACRE

*W*hen we arrived at the Brick Palace, the site of the attack, the paranormal police were already there. We got out of the truck, following Nero past a dozen police officers, every single one of them gaping at us as we entered the building. Well, we did look menacing in our black leather uniforms, but that was the point. The Legion was able to maintain order on Earth because everyone was afraid of us. That fear started with the black battle leather and weapons, but the outfits weren't everything. During the drive over here, Nero had lectured us on the importance of maintaining a menacing demeanor. No laughing or smiling or joking. We were supposed to walk around like we were ready to kill anyone at anytime. That was what gave the Legion its true power. The magic we had just allowed us to follow through on that silent promise.

We walked up the stairwell, passing forensic teams and corpses I was trying really hard not to see. Bodies were everywhere, so many bodies, their faces frozen in the moment of their death. I'd seen dead people before, but I'd never seen so many in one place. There were no wounds on their bodies, but just because this wasn't a bloodbath didn't mean it wasn't a massacre—or a harrowing experience. One moment these people had been walking around, and then the next they were dead, just like that.

Tightness tugged on my heart. I wanted to weep for these poor strangers, to let them know that someone cared about their passing, but I couldn't. I had to keep up my menacing appearance. The Legion didn't approve of breaking down into tears at the scene of a massacre. Nero's eyes, as hard as green diamonds, panned coolly across the corpses, not a hint of emotion in them. Jace and Mira weren't as cold as Nero, but they didn't appear to be on the verge of tears either. Their Legion parents had probably taught them to detach themselves from their humanity.

Every living person we passed paused to stare at Nero. He was a celebrity around these parts, the only angel in all of New York. Most people were enamored with angels, but the police knew better. They were obviously more scared than in awe of him. They'd probably dealt with the Legion often enough to realize the truth: angels were cold, vicious, and even more deadly than they were beautiful. I should really remind myself of that the next time I daydreamed about Nero.

"Detective," Nero said as he stopped in front of a man in a dark suit.

The rest of us stood behind Nero, his silent backup. Truth be told, we were really kind of superfluous next to an angel, but I had a feeling we were here to learn more than to actually do anything. As we stood there, I tried to keep my eyes hard, my body still, and my mouth shut. It was a battle against everything that I was.

"We weren't expecting you, Colonel," the detective said. He didn't look very happy about our arrival—ok, Nero's arrival. His wary eyes never flickered away from our fearless leader.

"Tell me what happened here," Nero said.

The Legion didn't make requests. They gave orders. And if you didn't obey those orders, there was no power on Earth that could save you. So while the detective bristled at the power behind Nero's command, he complied.

"The victims are all vampires, and they were poisoned," he said.

I hadn't even known you could poison a vampire.

"From what we can tell, someone tampered with the magic steam system used for heating and cooling the building," the detective continued. "They distributed the poison in the air. All eighty-two people died instantly. We're bringing the evidence back to the station for analysis."

"No, you're not," Nero said. "This is a Legion matter now. You will hand over all evidence to us, and your people will leave immediately. This whole building is being put under magic quarantine."

The detective opened his mouth to protest, then he snapped it shut. Obviously he'd thought better of arguing with an angel. "Tell everyone to pull out of the building," he told a police officer. "And to give all samples they've collected to the Colonel's team."

Everyone in the room stopped what they were doing. One of the forensics people, a woman with a high ponytail, handed me a small sealed plastic bag with white residue inside.

As I tucked the bag into the pocket of my pants, Nero turned to us and said, "Load the bodies into the truck."

But before we could move, an explosion rocked the building. The walls burst apart, pommeling us with rocky shards. Flames raged behind the broken walls, and they were spreading fast. Nero dashed toward the fire, using his magic to hold back the flames. But it wasn't enough. As more walls collapsed around us, the whole building groaned in pitiful protest.

Everyone ran for the exit, but we were four floors up. The stairwell had collapsed, and the fire escape was behind a curtain of flames. A second explosion shook the building. Wooden beams fell into our path, the wood engorged with crackling flames. The floor beneath our feet split. Holes opened up, one of them as large as a sofa.

"Over there!" I shouted to the panicking crowd. "Line up in front of the hole." I looked at Jace and Mira. "Jump down and catch the people I throw to you."

Mira rolled her eyes at being ordered around, but both she and Jace jumped down. I began picking up people, tossing them down. Jace and Mira caught them and pushed them toward the fire escape. When the last human was safely off this crumbling floor, I jumped down. Nero was still battling the flames up above, but I couldn't stop to worry about him. He was an angel and could take care of himself. The rest of us didn't have elemental magic to protect us from the fire. We had to get out of here.

But another explosion quaked the building. We zigzagged between the burning posts that fell all around us. It seemed Captain Somerset had been right after all. Practicing those obstacle courses again and again had come in handy.

The police had already made it through the fire exit, and the three of us headed there now. We ran, our feet so fast they barely touched the ground. Even so, the floor was crackling under the weight. With an ominous crunch, it split apart beneath our feet, swallowing us whole. We fell two floors. I rolled out of my landing and so did Mira, but Jace fell onto a burning wood post and hit his head. Fire raged all around his still body. Mira gaped in shock, pulling back from the flames. I pushed past her, slipping off my jacket. I leapt at Jace and hit him with my jacket to put out the flames on his body. Then I swung him over my shoulder and jumped over the fire again. Thank goodness for vampire strength. Back when I'd been a regular human, I never would have been able to lift him, let alone jump so high while carrying him.

I punched Mira in the arm to snap her out of her shocked state. We hurried outside onto the fire escape, running down the shaking metal steps to the ground. As soon as we were at a safe distance from the burning building, I set Jace down on the sidewalk. He'd recovered consciousness and was coughing up a storm, but besides that and some blistered skin, he appeared to be fine. I tossed him a healing potion, then stood up to stare at the building.

Nero had been inside for a long time. He might have been powerful, but even angels could be blown apart by explosives. I was just about to run back inside to look for him when he burst through a window. His wings were extended, the shimmering feathers a devastatingly beautiful mix of blue, green, and black feathers. He flew over the building, his wings beating in a steady rhythm as he blasted magic at the raging fire, trying to contain it before it spread further. It was mesmerizing to watch—his power against that of the raging wildfire. That was no mundane fire. Someone must have enchanted the flames. They were spreading too quickly, too mercilessly.

Firetrucks pulled up on the street, their lights flashing and sirens blaring. Two dozen men and women in rubber suits piled out of the trucks and hurried toward the building, blasting it with their magic. Streams of water and ice joined Nero's magic in the battle against the flames. The fire spat and sizzled in protest, countering with fiery whips, but after a few minutes under that constant barrage, the flames went out. As the water and ice elementals approached the smoking building, Nero landed beside us, his wings vanishing in a whiff of golden smoke as his feet touched down.

"My team has entered the building," a fireman wearing a headset told him.

"They will find nothing," replied Nero. "The fire consumed everything. The bodies are gone. The evidence is gone." He looked at us. "What do you have?"

I pulled out the plastic bag containing the residue the police had found. Surprisingly, the bag had survived. It was a good thing it had because that bag was the only evidence we had left.

"Someone didn't want you to investigate this," the detective commented.

"No, they didn't," Nero agreed, giving the building a dark look.

———

THE FIREFIGHTERS SAID THE BUILDING WASN'T STABLE, but that didn't stop Nero from going in anyway. The hard look in his eyes said he wasn't going to allow a collapsing building to keep him from figuring out who'd tried to blow us all to pieces. So while he proved how badass he really was, I waited outside with Jace and Mira. Apparently, we weren't invincible enough to go in with him. After a minute of standing with the silent staring twins, I was ready to take my chances with the collapsing building.

Unfortunately, I was supposed to behave myself and follow Nero's orders like the good little soldier I was most certainly not. I was smart enough to know my own mind and crazy enough to listen to it. The problem was my mind was feeling rather bipolar at the moment. We'd all just nearly died. One part of me felt this restless need to be doing something other than standing here. The other part, the rational part, reminded me I needed to behave if I ever wanted to receive the magic I needed to save my brother. Today, I listened to the rational part of my brain, which was truly every bit as exciting as it sounded.

Mira glared at me, as though it were my fault I'd witnessed her freezing up inside the building. Maybe she was afraid of fire or of collapsing buildings. If so, she clearly didn't want me to know about it. Weaknesses made a person human, and the children of angels prided themselves on their utter lack of humanity.

Jace wasn't glaring at me, but his stare was certainly unsettling. He was looking at me like warts had sprouted up all over my face. I slid my finger across my cheek and found only smooth skin still warm from our dash through the fire. And yet Jace continued to stare in silence. I'd just saved his life. The least he could have done was say thank you.

Insults were preferable to this silence. I wished he would just go back to making fun of me like he and the brats had been doing since I'd joined the Legion. After I'd rescued Nero from vampires on the Black Plains, my actions had shocked the brats enough that they'd given me a week of respite from the taunts. But as soon as that had worn off, they'd grown worse than ever before. One night, they'd even tried to jump me as I was returning from a run outside. My extra training with Nero had made me strong, but not stronger than two people who were descended from angels and had been training to join the Legion their whole lives. It was only by luck—and a bit of scrappy fighting I'd picked up from my days of living on the street—that I'd managed to knock them out. After that, I'd dragged them down the hall and deposited them inside Captain Somerset's office.

"Well, well, what do we have here?" she'd said, her lips curling up with amusement. "A kitten bringing me mice?"

"These *mice* tried to beat me senseless." And I'd had the bleeding lip to prove it.

"It appeared that plan backfired. Two against one and they still lost. How embarrassing. I don't think they'll try that again."

"Or they'll just bring more people next time." That's me, the eternal optimist.

"Then you'd better get practicing, Pandora. Have Nero teach you to fight with an electric whip."

So I had—and immediately regretted it as Nero demonstrated the electric whip by using it on me. He claimed this was the best way to learn, but I had a sinking suspicion he just liked to torture me. Every time he'd hit me with that electric whip, it had felt like I was being struck by lightning.

When I'd complained to Captain Somerset about her brilliant idea, she'd laughed and told me I had to learn to move faster. Eventually, I did. The next time the brats came for me, they brought three people. When I pulled out the electric whip, they'd been surprised—but not as surprised as they'd been when I'd defeated them again.

"Well done," Captain Somerset had laughed the second time I dragged unconscious brats into her office.

They hadn't attacked me since then, but I knew it was only a matter of time. I didn't wonder why the brats hated me. I'd humiliated them by standing up to their attacks— and winning. But what else could I have done? Lain down and let them beat me bloody?

"The Magitech in the whole building was out," a fireman told Nero as they walked up to us, breaking through my self-reflection. "That's why the sprinklers and other anti-fire measures weren't working. The explosions were centered around the Magitech generators in the building, so we suspect sabotage, but we didn't find any evidence of it. It must have all burned up in the explosions and resulting fires."

Nero nodded, waving his hand to dismiss the fireman. It was just the four of us now. Nero had commanded the police to leave half an hour ago, and the firefighters were all in and around the building. Nero looked at us, saying nothing. The silence dragged on.

"Someone poisoned a building full of vampires," I said, unable to take the silence any longer. "Then they torched this building to wipe out all evidence. They didn't want anyone to find out what had happened here."

"Yes," Nero said, his voice hard and low. "But we do have evidence. If I'm right, the residue you have in that bag is from the poison that killed the residents of this building. And we're going to track that poison back to the guilty party."

CHAPTER 4

IMMORTAL HEARTS

*B*y the time we got back to the Legion, it was our dinner hour. In fact, dinner was nearly over. Nero dismissed Jace and Mira. As they hurried off to the canteen, Nero turned his cold eyes on me. Was he getting ready for a lecture? I'd behaved myself today. Well, except for maybe giving him an irked look when he'd told me to stay put outside of the Brick Palace…and I'd spoken without permission a few—ok, a bunch of times. I was so bad at this. I smiled at him anyway. There was no situation a smile couldn't turn around, right?

Nero clearly disagreed with the sentiment. He met my smile with a disapproving slant to his mouth.

Well, excuse me for being nice. How horribly inappropriate of me.

"Take the residue sample to Dr. Harding in Lab One," he said. "As you wait for the results, I want you to watch how she runs the tests. Have her explain everything she does to you. When it's done, bring the results to me in my office."

My stomach growled in protest—and I almost did too. The tests would take hours, and I was starving now. I thought the cruel and unusual punishment was saved for the Legion's prisoners, not their soldiers.

Who are you kidding? my inner cynic said. *They've been torturing you for months. And you're just sitting back and taking it.*

I nodded to Nero and rushed down the hall before my dark side got me into trouble. Mouthing off to him would feel good while it lasted, but that feeling would be short-lived. I was too tired and hungry to argue with an angel, and I certainly didn't have the energy to spend the rest of the night enduring whatever punishment he came up with in response to my disobedience.

I ran up the stairs to the next floor, where all the labs were located. Maybe this wouldn't take hours. If I hurried, I might be able to swing by the canteen and snag some left-overs before they cleared everything away. With that ray of hope beaming inside of my mind, I burst through the door into Lab One.

"Where's the fire?" a woman in a lab coat asked, smirking at me. The name on her coat said Dr. Harding. Bingo.

"No fire." I sashayed over to the table she was standing behind, dropping the plastic bag containing the residue onto it. "We found this residue at the Brick Palace."

Her dark brows drew together. "The vampire house?"

"Yes, every vampire inside died by inhaling poison pumped through the cooling system."

"Lovely way to die," she said, frowning.

"We need to figure out what substance killed them."

Dr. Harding picked up the bag and peered through the plastic window at the residue. "You didn't bring me very much of it. And how about some bodies?"

I didn't think she was trying to be morbid. She simply

wanted to see how the people had died. Unfortunately, I couldn't help her with that.

"A few minutes after we got to the Brick Palace, explosions went off all over the building," I told her. "All the bodies burned up. The rest of the evidence too. We barely got out of there before we became the next victims."

She sighed. "I'll try to make do with what you brought me." She opened the bag, but when I didn't leave, her dark brown eyes darted up at me. "Why are you being a fly on the wall of my lab?"

Believe me, I wish I could leave. But I just said, "Nero ordered me to be a fly on the wall of your lab. I'm supposed to watch you and learn."

"*Nero*, you say?" she asked, her mouth curling in a combination of amusement and surprise. "Well, if the good Colonel is making you stand here and watch, by all means come closer. Maybe you'll learn something."

I closed up next to her at the table. "What does that do?" I asked, pointing at the Magitech machine she'd just flipped open. It looked like a simple glass box, but I knew that couldn't be all it was.

"It's going to analyze the magic in this residue."

She poured a pinch of the residue into a shallow bowl, then set the bowl into the machine. As soon as she closed the door, the whole thing lit up. She flipped on the glowing box, and it began to hum softly. A grid of red lights flickered rapidly all across the glassy surface. Slowly, light by light, the grid began to turn orange.

As it did its thing, I looked around the lab. My gaze snagged on a bowl of chocolate chip cookies sitting on the desk across the room, and my stomach let out a low, desperate roar.

"By all means, take as many as you want," Dr. Harding said, smiling.

I wasn't sure if she felt sorry for me or was just amused by me, but I found I didn't care as long as I got those cookies.

As many as I want? Why, I don't mind if I do.

It turned out there were only two cookies in that bowl, and I took them both. Before the lights on the machine had turned yellow, those cookies were gone, and my stomach was begging for more food. A quick survey of the lab's contents let me know that unless I wanted to sample the mysterious objects floating in jars on the bookshelves, then my stomach was out of luck until I could get out of here.

"Still hungry?" Dr. Harding asked.

"I haven't eaten since breakfast, and I don't even know how many calories I've burned since then."

"Ah, the early training days." She said the words without a hint of nostalgia.

"You sound glad to be done with those days," I told her.

"Oh, you have the wrong idea there, dear… What's your name?"

"Leda Pierce."

Her eyes widened.

"I take it you've heard of me," I said drily.

"Oh, yes." Her mouth twisted into a delighted smile. "I most certainly have." But before I could ask her what she'd heard about me, she continued, "You're never done with training, Leda. Once a quarter, we all have to complete another training course. The Legion wants each and every one of their soldiers to be able to kill anything in their path without problem or pause."

"Even the scientists?"

"Even the scientists."

"Dr. Harding—"

"Oh, no, you simply must call me Nerissa. After what you've done…" She was grinning.

"What did I do?"

"You traveled across the Black Plains to rescue Nero Windstriker."

"Oh, that."

"Yes, *that*. You rescued an angel, dear. That's not something people around here forget." She leaned her elbows on the table, balancing her chin on her hands. "So, how was it?"

"Black and cloudy. The Black Plains have been scorched for two hundred years. Every living thing is touched by that magic. Even the trees are black."

"No, not the Black Plains." She gave her hand a dismissive wave, as though there were nothing interesting about a plain of monsters. "How was it being out there with Colonel Windstriker?"

"Uh, well, it was dangerous. And he told me off for coming after him."

Nerissa chuckled softly. "Of course he did. But he must have appreciated it anyway."

"If you call appreciation two hours of extra running every evening for a month."

"To an angel, dear, that's merely foreplay."

I was stunned to silence.

"You train with him every day," she continued.

"Where did you hear that?"

She shrugged. "Everyone is talking about it."

"But no one even knows who I am," I protested.

"They do now," she said brightly. "Once Colonel Windstriker made his intentions clear, you became famous here."

"What intentions?" I said, almost afraid to ask.

"His intentions to make you his lover, of course."

Yep, I should have listened to my inner voice. It was right. I really didn't want to know.

"I…uh…" I stuttered stupidly.

She smiled at me.

"That's not what's happening," I told her, my cheeks flushed. "Nero is not trying to make me his lover."

"Of course not, dear. Angels don't try to make someone their lover. They just do it. So, did you go after him on the Black Plains because you thought that would pique his interest, or was that just a happy coincidence?"

"This is not a *happy* coincidence," I muttered, trying to keep the growl out of my voice.

"Ah, so it was intentional." She nodded, obviously missing my emphasis. "I thought so. As far as plans to catch his attention go, that's the boldest one I've heard."

"Why in heaven would anyone want to catch Nero's attention?" I demanded. "Especially when the only way to catch his attention is to do something that will incur his wrath?"

"Well, it worked for you," she said.

"Nothing worked. I rescued him because it was the right thing to do, not so that he'd sleep with me."

"But that doesn't mean you don't want to sleep with him."

"I…" My heart let out a heavy thump, betraying me.

Since Nerissa had the same amplified hearing as I did, she heard it too. "I thought so," she said, smiling knowingly. "Don't worry. I promise I won't tell anyone."

I looked around for an escape from this conversation, but there was none. The earth couldn't even be bothered to open up beneath my feet and swallow me whole. Where was an impending apocalypse when you really needed one?

"But I think people know. Everyone is watching you," she said. "You're famous."

Well, that was certainly the opposite of comforting. "Any chance my new-found fame can score me some more cookies?" I asked her, trying to divert the conversation away from this awful subject.

"If I give you some more, will you talk to Nero about my request for additional lab equipment?"

"I think you'll have better luck talking to him yourself."

"I already did. He called my request frivolous. But if his lover talked to him…"

"I am *not* his lover."

"Give it a few weeks. Or days. Then you can bring forth my proposal. Bring it up when he's in the throes of passion." She grinned at me. "You'll have better luck that way."

I ground my teeth together. No cookies were worth this. The magic-analyzing machine took that moment to beep, thereby saving me from any further discussions with the doctor about Nero's throes of passion.

"Ok, it's finished," Nerissa said, serious again. "Now let's see what kind of magic we're dealing with."

———

ON THE PLUS SIDE, AS SOON AS THE MACHINE WAS DONE, Nerissa was so busy with the slew of other tests she wanted to perform on the residue that she didn't have time to talk about me and Nero doing the horizontal tango. On the not-so-plus side, those tests took *hours*. By the time we were done, not only was the canteen closed, but all of the kitchen staff were done for the day too. There would be no late night munchies for me.

I headed for Nero's office, hoping that my hunger

wouldn't make me snap at him. The least he could have done was let me swing by Demeter for some food before I'd headed to the lab. But no, soldiers of the Legion could go days without eating, so how about we test that?

By the time I made it to Nero's office, I was bitter, angry, and famished—and I let the door know it. When he didn't respond to my hard knocks, I tried again. Nothing. I pulled on the handle, but it was locked.

"Nero isn't here."

I turned around. Across the hall from Nero's office, Captain Somerset stood in the doorway of her own office. It was a good thing she wasn't telepathic because the curses that blared through my head would have made her ears bleed. My hands shook so hard that I nearly lost a grip on the folder in my hands. He'd made me sit through all of that while starving, and he couldn't even be bothered to wait for my report? He'd probably gone off to satisfy his own late night munchies.

"Nero is in his apartment. Take that up to him," she said, nodding at the folder in my hands.

"Can't I just give it to you?" I asked. I was afraid that if I saw Nero right now, I wouldn't be able to hold my tongue.

She chuckled and closed her door. Well, that was answer enough. Up to the angel's lair it was.

The top-ranked Legion officers in New York had their apartments on the highest floor of the building. I spent the seemingly endless climb up the stairs trying to concentrate on what Nerissa had told me about the residue. She'd used a lot of weird science-y words I didn't know the meaning of, so replaying what she'd said confused my brain. I'd take it. Better to meet Nero in a state of confusion than in a state of rage.

I knocked on his apartment door and waited. I considered the consequences of giving Nero a lecture about cruel and unusual punishment. I decided it was worth the risk— but the words evaporated from my tongue the moment he answered the door. He was wearing a pair of running pants. His complementary black tank top was cut low in the front and on the sides, showing off his arms and chest. Ok, I admit it. I stopped and stared. Gaped even. My eyes traced the damp sheen that coated his body, like he'd just been working out.

"Yes?"

I tore my eyes off of—well, everything—and settled my gaze on an empty patch of air over his right shoulder. Nerissa's confident lilt, that promise that I'd be Nero's lover, sang in my mind. I silenced that song by dropping a mountain of sheer stubbornness onto it.

"I have the lab report," I said, my voice uneven. Damn it.

"Come in," he said, stepping aside to allow me to pass.

I did, my gaze flickering to the new addition to his apartment as he closed the door. He'd installed a salmon ladder just like the one in Captain Somerset's obstacle course. Last week, I'd walked into the gym to find him tackling that obstacle. He'd done it topless too, much to the appreciation of his admiring female audience. Just thinking back on it still gave me goosebumps. His fierce fluidity. The way beads of sweat had slid between the ridges of his muscles…

I slammed down a big barrier, blocking out those images.

Nero stood opposite me, hopefully completely unaware of my wicked fantasies. I pressed my thighs together and clutched the folder. He held out his hand. I took an immediate step forward, then froze, realizing that he wasn't beckoning me forward. He just wanted the lab report. Blushing, I handed it to him.

Pull yourself together, I chided myself as Nero opened the folder and began to read. I considered leaving, but he hadn't dismissed me yet, so I had a feeling I was expected to just stand there. While I waited, the hungry part of me wondered if the kitchen was unlocked. Maybe I could sneak some food from the pantry.

Nero looked up from the page. "What did you learn about the residue?"

I blinked, confused. "The report is right there."

He stiffened. Oops. He must have thought I was talking back. Again.

"I just meant, I thought you wanted the official report," I said quickly.

"I have Dr. Harding's report. Now I want to hear *yours.*"

Great. "Dr. Harding found traces of Sunset Pollen and Snapdragon Venom in the residue. They are, uh, substances recently engineered by witches," I said.

"Go on."

I babbled for a minute, trying to talk my way through some of the stuff Nerissa had told me, but I didn't really understand most of it, so I probably got half of the terms wrong. The ordeal was made even more difficult by the fact that Nero was watching me the whole time.

He continued to stare at me for a few silent seconds after I was done talking, then he said, "I will get you some books so you can read up on magic forensics. And chemistry. And magical science in general."

"How big will this stack of books be?"

"Only as big as it needs to be," he told me.

Knowing Nero, that meant a ten-foot stack of books. I hoped my roommates didn't mind that I'd soon have to use their beds as bookshelves. I sighed.

Nero seemed to gather the gist of my thoughts. "You

need this knowledge. You cannot advance further in the Legion without it."

"I'm still working on the vampire skills. And you want to pile on witchy stuff now?"

"You wanted me to help you advance quickly, and this is how it works. Did you think this would be easy?"

No, not really. The Legion of Angels wasn't known for its easygoing attitude. He was right. If I wanted to find my brother Zane, I had to work harder. And I had to work fast. Wherever my brother was now, he seemed safe, but it was only a matter of time before either the gods or the demons found him and exploited him for his power.

"With each level in the Legion, you need to improve your current skills *and* the new ones," Nero continued on. "It's a constant effort to better yourself."

I glanced at the salmon ladder in his living room. My head panned up the many levels of metal. It was a good thing his ceiling was so high. It looked like he was striving too.

"It all sounds so exhausting," I commented.

"It is." He walked over to the bookcases that covered one wall. He pulled out a book in a single, crisp movement, as though he knew exactly where every book on his shelves was. "Start with this one while I prepare a list for you from the library."

I glanced down at the front cover. It was a basic monotone blue background with the title written in white block letters. *The Basics of Magical Chemistry*, was it? There was nothing basic about it. The book weighed more than the weights Nero had been making me bench press. I'd hate to see the followup book.

"I'm too exhausted for mental gymnastics right now," I told him. "I haven't even eaten yet."

"Then let's take care of that."

Smooth as a silk ribbon on the wind, he moved over to the dining room table, which I only now realized was set for dinner. Dinner for one. Nero placed a second plate and set of silverware across from the first. Oh gods, was Nerissa right? Was he trying to seduce me?

"I didn't expect the lab analysis to take so long," Nero said.

"Is this an apology?"

He shot me a hard look. Ok, apparently not. He probably thought apologies were for people too stupid to make the right choice the first time. Yeah, that would totally be Nero logic.

"I was working in my office. By the time I realized how late it was, the canteen was closed," he said. "So I had the kitchen staff send some food up to me." He lifted the lid from a very large platter, revealing a dinner that could have easily left four people stuffed. "They always send way too much," he said in response to my gaping eyes. If I hadn't known better, I'd have sworn a hint of sheepishness flashed across his face. But it couldn't be. That was an emotion unbefitting of an angel.

He pulled a wine bottle and two glasses from the other side of the bar that separated the kitchen from the dining room. Wine too? All that was missing were the candles and the mood music. The reasonable, rational part of me battled it out with the little tramp who wondered what it would be like to pour that wine all over Nero's chest and then lick it up. I was frozen in place, caught between running toward him and fleeing the other way.

"Do I need to order you to sit down and eat?" he demanded with a hint of impatience as he sat.

The purely callous way that he said it allowed hunger to finally tip the scales. This wasn't about seducing me. This was about feeding me so he could torture me again tomorrow. Expelling an internal sigh of relief, I took the seat across from his.

As soon as I was seated, the three candles on the table flickered to life, and the room lighting dimmed. My mind flashed back to the last time I'd been in his room with candles lit all around us—and to the blood exchange we'd done so that I could catch a glimpse of my brother by linking to Zane through Nero's magic. Just the sight of Nero's blood had turned me into a crazy nymphomaniac who made that little tramp inside of me—the one who'd wanted to lick wine off of Nero earlier—look like a saint. Thinking about Nero's blood now sent a rush of heat through my entire body.

I crossed my ankles, folded my hands, and most certainly did not watch the shift of muscle in Nero's arms as he poured the wine. I cleared my throat, trying to clear my mind of wicked intentions too. If those thoughts made their way to Nero, he might punish me. Or worse yet, he might play out my darkest desires. What was with the candles anyway? Was he trying to seduce me or test me? I drew in a deep breath to steady my nerves, but my own scent betrayed the need burning inside of me. But at least my fangs didn't descend this time, which meant I was starting to get *some* control over them.

I winked at Nero. "I always knew you wanted to ask me out on a date," I said, trying to cover my sudden mood shift with a joke.

"Is that what this is?" he said, his voice perfectly neutral.

"Uh…" I reached for the dinner rolls just to have something to do with my hands. Nero filled my glass with wine.

"Trying to get me drunk, angel?"

His face remained impassive. "That's not hard."

"It's Nectar that gets me drunk. I can hold my liquor," I boasted.

———

Two bottles of wine later, I was eating my words. I'd have been eating Nero's words too if he'd only asked. But though he'd drunk one of those two bottles himself, he looked no different than usual. I, on the other hand, was so relaxed that I was practically melting into his sofa. We'd moved there after a dinner that had left me satisfyingly stuffed.

I'd just finished telling him the story of the time Zane and I had chased an escaped thief through the town's sewage system. We'd caught him, but by then we'd stunk so badly that Calli wouldn't let us enter the house until we stripped down in the front yard and she shot us with a high-pressure hose. She'd burned our clothes. As I finished the story, Nero's mouth thinned into a hard line.

"Ok, so maybe that wasn't the most appropriate story I could have told you, but I do have worse ones. It wasn't the only time I had to go through the sewers," I said. "But I guess an angel would never do something so uncouth."

"You would be surprised at what uncouth things I've done in my life, both before and after I got my wings."

Now we were getting somewhere. "Do tell," I said, leaning forward eagerly.

"Perhaps another time."

"You're such a tease."

"I'll answer one of your questions if you answer one of mine."

"Ok, I'll play." I grinned at him. "What have I got to lose? You already know my biggest secret. Ask away."

He didn't waste time. "Is there something between you and Zane?"

"Not blood, if that's what you mean. I told you we're not related."

"I remember." He looked into my eyes for a few long moments, as though he were trying to read something in them.

"Then what…" I snorted. "Oh, *that*. I don't have the hots for him if that's what you mean. He might not be my brother by blood, but he is my brother in my heart."

Nero remained silent, his face etched in marble.

"Wow, that was a really silly thing to waste your question on," I told him. "You must be miffed."

"Alcohol makes you bold," he said.

I arched my brows at him. "The question is, does it make *you* bold?"

"No, angels are immune to mundane alcohol. I just like the taste of wine."

I chuckled, rubbing my hands together with glee. "Now to come up with a really good question."

"You already used your question," he informed me coolly.

"When did I…" I frowned. "You mean when I asked you if alcohol made you bold? That doesn't count. I didn't mean for that to be my question."

"Whether you meant it or not, you asked it. And rules are rules."

"But—"

"That was a really silly thing to waste your question on," he cut in. "You must be miffed."

I folded my arms across my chest and glared at him. "Suddenly, this game isn't fun anymore. You play mean."

"The game has always been the same," he said. "You're just now beginning to understand the rules."

What did that even mean? I was too drunk to try to figure it out.

"The Legion is about pushing yourself beyond your limits," he told me. "And when your limits grow, you push against those too. Again and again. That is the secret to gaining the gods' gifts, the secret to leveling up your magic."

"So, basically, you're telling me the gods reward the stubborn and the restless."

A small smile twisted his lips. "I suppose that's one way of putting it."

"I know how much you love to teach by example." I glanced at the salmon ladder. "Care to use your new toy to offer a demonstration of this stubborn, restless quality the Legion needs in its soldiers?" I tried to keep a straight face. Since I was smashed, I probably failed.

"Ladies first," he said with perfect politeness.

"Uh, no. I think I've had too much to drink for that. The bar would slip right off the edge." My hand flew to my forehead. "Then hit me in the head."

"That would be a valuable lesson. You must be ready to fight anywhere, anytime."

"If vampires storm the room, I'm sure you can hold them off while I nap," I said, brushing a strand of hair from his face.

He caught my hand, magic rippling across our connection. "You let your guard down too easily."

"And you don't let it down easily enough," I shot back.

In a flash, he had my arms pinned to the sofa. He leaned in to whisper against my ear, "You must be ready for battle at any time."

"Not against you, you crazy angel. You're on my side."

The hot kiss of his breath felt too good, so good that even I in my inebriated state knew I was in trouble if I didn't get free of him. I pushed against his hold, but he was too strong. "Let me go." I tried to kick him. He trapped my leg easily.

"You must always be ready," he said. "A threat can come from anywhere, even from the place you least expect it. Stay alert. Don't trust anyone."

"Even you?" I asked, shoving against his unbreakable hold.

A dark look shone in his eyes. "Especially me."

I wasn't making any more progress in freeing myself than I had this morning when he'd trapped me during our one-on-one training session. My arms and legs were pinned, and he was too far away for me to head-butt him. This called for drastic measures. I turned my neck and bit down on my own shoulder. As my blood rose to the surface, Nero's eyes widened, a blue-silver sheen sliding over them, masking his natural emerald color. That moment of distraction cost him. I pushed him off of me and retreated to the other side of the living room. Adrenaline kicked in, shooting my heightened metabolism into high gear. The haze of alcohol began to clear from my mind.

Nero shook his hands, as though freeing himself from the mesmerizing effect of my blood. "That was a dirty trick."

"Says he who got me drunk and then attacked me to prove a point. Why does everything with you have to be a test?"

"Tests help you push yourself to new limits."

He moved in so quickly that one moment he was standing by the sofa, and the next he was right in front of me. He swung a punch at me, but he was slower than usual, and I evaded it.

"Let me heal your neck. It's distracting," he told me. Well, that explained his slowness.

I dipped my finger in the stream of blood dripping down my neck. "You must always stay alert, no matter what distractions are around you." Smirking, I held out my finger.

"I'm *very* alert right now." His eyes followed the stream of my blood down to my collarbone. Raw need burned in his eyes. He wanted my blood every bit as much as I wanted his, and I was going to use that to my advantage.

Or not. He might have been slower than usual, but he was still too fast. He caught my hand as I attacked, twisting my arm behind me. I tried to power out of his hold, but my back slammed into his chest.

"Well, this is nice," I commented.

He didn't dignify my flippancy with a response. Instead, he wrapped one arm more tightly around me, even as he traced his finger down my neck to my shoulder. His hand settled there, and a gentle warmth spread across my body, healing my wound. Then his mouth lowered to my neck, and he let out a slow breath.

A shudder rippled down my spine. My body jerked as his breath melted into my skin, drowning me in a rush of savage longing. I could feel my blood awakening with fire, rising up to him. His mouth dipped lower, and his tongue flicked out to lick the blood from my neck.

"Bite me," I said, my voice somewhere between a rasp and a moan.

"I just healed you," Nero said, but he slid my ponytail off my shoulder, clearing my neck.

I tilted my head to give him easy access to my throat. His mouth closed over my throbbing vein, but his fangs didn't descend. He sucked hard, drinking in the blood still wet on my skin. A wave of fevered desire tore through me, consuming me from the inside out.

"Please," I shuddered, reaching back to pull him closer to me.

I could sense every muscle in his body tensing as he teetered on the edge of losing control. "I shouldn't." His hand stroked down my arm, his touch feather-light.

A knock sounded on the door, and Nero dropped his hands from me, pulling back. With the heat of his body gone, I was left cold and shivering. I turned around to face him. His eyes were panning across the apartment at the mess we'd made during our short fight.

"Go to the other room," he said so quietly I could hardly hear him. He pointed at a closed door off to the side of the living room.

"Who is it?" I asked in the same volume.

"The First Angel."

Those three words froze what little heat still lingered inside of me. I didn't think the First Angel would be happy to find me in Nero's apartment—or to learn what we'd been doing here.

Nero walked toward the front door, the furniture settling back into place behind him. His perfect control over his psychic magic was both amazing and terrifying. It was one thing to blast someone across the room with raw power, and Nero certainly had raw power to spare. But the subtle control of silently moving the furniture around was quite another thing. I paused in the doorway to watch him for a moment, then I ducked into the room. My curiosity got the better of me, so I kept the door cracked open just enough to see.

Why had the First Angel come to see Nero here so late in the night? A knot formed in my stomach. I hoped she wasn't looking for a little nocturnal angel-on-angel fun. Nero opened the door to his apartment, bowing, and Nyx glided past him with all the beauty and grace of an angel.

"I've read Dr. Harding's report on the residue," she said straight away, all business. "Sunset Pollen and Snapdragon Venom." Her blue eyes pulsed once. "Both substances were recently developed by the witches of the New York University of Witchcraft. They are still highly experimental, and thus the witches do not allow them off the university's grounds. My advisers want me to arrest every single person in the school."

"Impractical," Nero decided after half a second. "That is over two thousand people. There is no way we could secure them all. As soon as we started rounding up witches, both the innocent and the guilty alike would flee. That's just human nature."

Nyx's mouth twitched. "It is indeed. Colonel Fireswift proposes we arrange an assembly for all students and faculty, then capture everyone at once."

"With all due respect to Colonel Fireswift, that is an idiotic plan. The students and faculty make up most of the school's numbers, but not all. There are gardeners, janitors, and all manner of other staff. How does he propose we invite them too without arousing suspicion?"

"He doesn't. Colonel Fireswift does not believe any of them could possibly be responsible."

"That's where he's wrong. You might need to be a witch to create potions and magic bombs, but you don't need a sliver of supernatural blood in you to use many of them."

"I agree with you, Nero. In our arrogance, we angels often forget that it doesn't require great power to be capable of great evil." Nyx sighed. "Besides, even if we caught the guilty party, I'm not sure we'd know it. I haven't yet been able to get anything out of the last witches we captured. The demons put magic safeguards on them. They don't break under torture. We're still looking for a way to shatter that spell."

"You believe the demons are pulling the strings this time too?" Nero asked her.

"I cannot ignore the possibility. Why would anyone but a demon want to kill a building full of vampires?"

Nero's eyes flashed with understanding. "You think it was a sacrifice."

"We won't know until we figure out who's behind this. That residue is our only clue, and it's pointing at the New York University of Witchcraft. I need you to find a way to investigate how those two substances made it out of the school's labs. But do it carefully. Otherwise, the guilty party will flee, and if the demons give them sanctuary in hell, we won't know it. We might never get to the bottom of this. Covert is the key word here."

That key word was the complete opposite of the standard Legion solution to their problems: charging in swords drawn, guns blazing, blasting down doors.

"I will prepare a mission plan," Nero said.

Nyx nodded. She was turning to leave when she looked down, her eyes focusing on a tiny drop of blood on the white marble floor. She paused and looked around. The furniture was all in order, but two empty bottles of wine still sat on the dining room table.

"Late night drink, Colonel?" she asked, her perfectly-sculpted dark brows lifting.

Nero's face was as hard as his marble floor. "Something to unwind before bed."

Nyx continued to stare at the bottles for a moment, then she turned, stepping over the drop of blood on her way to the door. "I expect your mission plan first thing in the morning," she told him before she left.

Nero locked the door behind her. I stayed where I was, just in case Nyx was still nearby. Nero must have been thinking the same thing. He crossed the living room with silent steps, then slowly peeled back the door I'd been hiding behind the whole time.

"You were eavesdropping," he whispered, noting how close I was to the door.

I shrugged and smiled, and as I turned around, I realized where I was.

"You hid me in your bedroom?" I hissed under my breath. "Why don't you just stuff me under your bed like a dirty magazine?"

"I would have, but I didn't think you'd go quietly."

Anger surged through me until I caught that tiny twitch at the corner of his mouth. "Are you *mocking* me?" I demanded.

"Of course not."

I clenched my jaw. "You *are* mocking me."

"Leda, it was either my bedroom or the bathroom."

My gaze flickered to the bed, and I suddenly remembered what we'd been doing before Nyx had knocked on the door. "I have to go," I said, turning to hide my burning face. "I need to get to bed if I'm going to be able to get up for our training session in a few hours."

"We'll have to skip tomorrow's training. I have a report to get ready for Nyx."

He looked like he wanted to say something more, like he was also thinking about what we'd been doing earlier. But maybe I was just projecting. I nodded and hurried past him, leaving the apartment before I could succumb to temptation. I didn't slow down until I reached the stairwell.

Nero's an angel, I thought as I descended the stairs. *Can I trust him?*

Oddly enough, the first answer that sprang into my mind was a resounding *yes*. He knew about Zane's magic, a magic the gods we served would exploit for their own gain without any thought for Zane's well-being, but he hadn't told anyone. He hadn't betrayed my trust. And he never would. Somehow, I was sure of it. I could trust him, at least when it came to helping me save Zane.

But I couldn't trust him with my heart. Captain Somerset had told me about the many immortal hearts Nero had broken in his many immortal years. And if Nerissa was right, I was next in line. But it didn't have to be that way. I could stop this now, before it began. I didn't have time for a broken heart. I'd already suffered through enough heartache in my past. Nero was helping me, but I wasn't under any delusions. He was an angel, and angels didn't think like other people. They didn't see others in the same way. Some key part of humanity was missing from them.

This was only a physical attraction between me and Nero —that and nothing else. He wanted me, I wanted him. We'd have world-shattering sex. Maybe it would last a few happy weeks, or maybe even months. I'd probably fall for him. I kept my heart guarded, but Nero was the sort of man who could break through those guards. And once I fell, I'd fall hard. Eventually, though, he would grow bored of my humanity, and then that would be that. He'd leave me to pick up the pieces of my shattered heart.

No, I wouldn't do it. I couldn't be broken when I needed to help Zane. So I had to stay detached from that fiercely beautiful angel. I had to resist him, no matter how much I didn't want to.

CHAPTER 5

SOMETHING WICKED

*B*right and early the next morning, I took an extended shower, then headed down to the canteen. Thanks to my newly heightened metabolism, I wasn't feeling the aftereffects of last night's wine. Though I missed many of the things I'd had to give up when I joined the Legion, hangovers were most certainly not one of them.

I didn't have a training session with Nero today, so for the first time in weeks, I had time for a long, leisurely breakfast with my friends. And I intended to make the best of it. I started off with two donuts, and I only got more ambitious from there.

"Are you really going to eat all of that?" Ivy asked, her brown eyes flickering to my fully-loaded food tray.

"Of course." I sat down across from her. "Where's Drake?"

"Captain Somerset summoned him away on a raid of some vampire hideout outside the city. You didn't hear her because you were singing in the shower at the time." Her brows lifted, inviting me to elucidate my bright spirits.

"I'm just happy I can have an actual breakfast this morning rather than the usual five-minute variety."

"Oh, is that all? I thought it had something to do with your visit to the Colonel's apartment last night." Her lips spread into a knowing smile, and she winked at me, her long eyelashes kissing her cheekbones.

"That was about work," I said, trying not to think about all the non-work things that had happened in his apartment.

"It must have been a lot of work. You were there for hours."

"How can you possibly… Never mind, I'm not surprised. You always know everything that's going on at the Legion."

Ivy slid her knife through her melon, cutting off a piece. "So are you going to make me ask you what happened in his apartment?"

"I gave him the lab report on the residue sample from the Brick Palace."

Ivy nodded. Of course she knew about the poisoning and bombing of the building I'd visited with Nero yesterday. It's all anyone around here was talking about right now. They were calling it the New York Massacre.

"And then?" Ivy prompted when I didn't continue.

I skewered a piece of pancake on my fork. "And then we ate a little."

"Dinner?" Her eyes lit up. "You had dinner with Nero Windstriker?"

"It's not like that. I hadn't eaten since breakfast, and the canteen was closed. He'd ordered up some food, and he let me have some. Probably so I wouldn't try to eat him. I was so starving."

"And did you?" Her lip twitched. "Eat him?"

"What?" My confusion melted away to embarrassment.

"No! Of course not. There was no angel eating. Steak, pota-toes, baby carrots."

"Dessert?"

I narrowed my eyes at her. "I'm talking about food, Ivy. Not sex."

She sighed. "Too bad."

I didn't share everything that had happened after dinner. That would just make things worse. Instead, I said, "I was talking to Nerissa Harding yesterday in the lab."

"Oh, I love her. She's so much fun. Though some people find her a bit…"

"Unfiltered?" I suggested.

"Yeah. She doesn't hold back."

"She wasn't holding back last night either. She told me that…that everyone thinks Nero…well, that he'd broadcast his intentions to make me his lover."

Milk shot out of Ivy's nose. She grabbed a napkin, drying the mess. "Sorry, I was just picturing what your face must have looked like when she said that."

"Is it true? Are people really saying that?"

"Yeah, they are. Sorry." Ivy gave me a pitying look. She knew how much I hated being the center of attention. But I wasn't a fan of pity either.

"Well, it doesn't matter what they say because it's not happening," I told her, standing. "Come on. We're going to be late for training."

Ivy didn't say anything more about it, and by the time we made it to Hall Four, we were deep in a conversation about Lieutenant Diaz, her latest admirer. Our cheerful chatter died down the moment we opened the door to find the obstacle course from hell waiting for us. Since Captain Somerset was away on a mission, her friend Sergeant Claudia Vance was in charge of training us today. Sergeant Vance had a tall, strong figure, but she'd somehow managed to keep her voluptuous curves beneath all that battle-hardened muscle. A long blonde braid hung over her shoulder like a whip, contrasting with her black workout suit. She looked like an ancient battle maiden in modern clothing.

By the end of the day, I'd decided that while she shared Captain Somerset's tough style, neither of them had perfected their training torture techniques as well as Nero. I hoped that wasn't a prerequisite skill to becoming an angel because I didn't think I had it in me to be that cruel.

Drake joined me and Ivy in Demeter right as we were sitting down to dinner. As always, he was in a great mood. Nothing seemed to dampen his spirits, not even a day-long mission chasing vampires.

"So, how was your mission?" I asked him as he sat down with a tray piled high with meat—and little else.

"Famishing." He grinned. "We were walking the whole day. The building was empty, but there was a secret door in the back that led into a tunnel system. Dark, stinky tunnels. Dead animals everywhere. Animal excrement everywhere. Animal hair everywhere."

"Sounds appetizing," Ivy said, pushing her tray away.

"Oh, it was disgusting all right. Water had flooded larger parts of the tunnels, and it wasn't clean water either. I think it must have leaked off the sewage system."

"Well, thank you for showering before you came to dinner," Ivy said, then resumed eating her dinner.

I didn't smell anything coming off of Drake except for the fresh scent of soap and a hint of spice from his cologne.

"Did you fight any vampires?" I asked him.

"No, but we did get to fight some giant sewer rats."

"Exciting," I said.

He grinned. "It really was. And in one of the tunnels, we

found pieces of glass. They seemed to be from broken potion vials. There was an old campsite site next to the glass. Blood was splattered across the walls and ground, and in the center of it all, we found five dead vampires."

"Charming."

"Oh, that's not the best part," he told me. "The blood wasn't from the dead vampires. It was witch blood. It looks like there was a fight between witches and vampires, and the vampires lost."

"How did they die?" I asked.

"They were poisoned, then burned. And get this: we found a powdery residue too. When we brought it to Dr. Harding, she told us it's the same residue that you guys found yesterday at the Brick Palace."

"Why did the witches kill the vampires?" Ivy asked.

Drake shrugged. "We don't know."

"That doesn't bode well for the witches," I said.

They gave me a curious look.

"The Legion believes it's witches behind the mass poisoning yesterday, specifically the witches of the New York University of Witchcraft. We found two substances in the residue, both of which could only have come from the university. They are new experimental elements they're developing."

"Well, it looks like the witches are developing more than just new elements," said Drake. "They're developing a revolution."

"Something wicked is brewing in New York," Ivy agreed. Her gaze dropped to the book I'd opened beside my food tray. "*The Basics of Magical Chemistry*? Why are you reading that?"

"My personal trainer says I have to cram all of this knowledge into my head," I told her.

"Your personal trainer? You mean Colonel Sexy Pants?"

I frowned. "He's not so sexy when he slams your head against the wall. Repeatedly."

"But whatever he's doing with you, you're getting better. I saw you take on Jace this morning. You were holding your own. No, more than that. You were kicking his ass."

That was an exaggeration. I'd only beaten Jace because I didn't have a problem using anything within reach as a weapon—and there had been a lot of things within reach in the gym.

"Nero says I still depend too much on my scrappy fighting. He says it's not dignified."

"But it *is* smart," Drake said. "You're resourceful, Leda. Learn all you can about dignified fighting from Colonel Windstriker, but keep your resourcefulness. Being a soldier of the Legion is about more than our bodies. It's about our brains too. He knows that."

"Yeah, he knows. Hence the homework." I thumped the book. "I tried reading during our break this afternoon. After staring at all these formulas and swiggly symbols for like an hour, I can tell you I don't feel very smart at all. I feel like the biggest moron on Earth. It's giving me a headache, and I'm not even absorbing a fraction of the material."

"How about a break to clear your head?" Ivy suggested.

"No time. I have to learn this." A heavy sigh shook my chest as I glanced down at the book. "Somehow."

"Just do your best and fudge the rest," Ivy said.

"I don't think that will work. Nero is going to give me a test. I know he is. There's *always* a test with him."

Like that 'test' last night in his apartment. He'd tried to prove I shouldn't let my guard down in front of anyone by getting me drunk and then attacking me. Who even did something like that? Oh, a crazy angel, that's who.

I'd always preferred to have faith in the humanity of people rather than write them off all as monsters, but Nero was right about one thing: trusting people had gotten me into a lot of trouble. Like what had happened with Harker. I'd trusted him, and he'd turned around and tried to sell me out to a god.

Nero was right about more things than I cared to admit to myself. I did have to study to get strong, to gain enough magic to help Zane. I stared down the fat book, silently promising it that I would conquer it.

"What you need is caffeine," Ivy told me.

"What I need is to throw this gargantuan book at Nero Windstriker," I muttered.

"I'm sure we can work additional weightlifting into your training."

I glanced back to find Nero standing behind me. Of course he was. He was always right there to watch me when I put my foot in my mouth. I shot him a wide smirk, using it to cover my embarrassment at being overheard.

"Will I be throwing you or will you be throwing me?" I asked.

The look he gave me was dangerous and dark, devastating and delicious—all wrapped up into one deadly combination.

Ivy jumped to her feet. "Uh, we have to go…do some pushups together." She grabbed Drake's hand, pulling him along with her out of the canteen.

I watched with surprise as Nero sat down opposite me. I could almost hear the collective shock of several hundred soldiers of the Legion. Angels didn't sit down here at this end of the room with the common foot soldiers. I was surprised the bench didn't collapse under the weight of his profound holiness.

Nero didn't seem to care that people were openly staring

at us. He folded his hands together on the tabletop and watched me.

"Ok, what is it? Do I have something in my teeth?" I asked him.

His eyes flickered to the book. "You've learned the first four chapters."

Well, *learned* was probably the wrong word. Made it through the first four chapters was more like it. I didn't understand half of what I'd read. Not that I was going to let on about my inadequacy. I'd just reread the chapters again later. Surely, they had to make more sense the second time around.

So I just faked it. "I hope my progress is satisfactory."

"That remains to be seen when I test you."

"I *knew* there would be a test," I grumbled.

He continued on. "I'm thinking essay questions. Ten of them. Two pages per question. And you'll have to draw diagrams of course."

"Essay questions…" I stopped, the brief flash of delight in his eyes giving him away. I laughed. "You're messing with me."

"I would never do such a thing," he said seriously.

I grinned at him. "You would and you are."

"I'm afraid you are mistaken, Pandora. But, unfortunately, your test will have to wait for another time."

"Oh?" I asked, trying not to sound too excited.

"The First Angel would like an audience with you."

CHAPTER 6

THE FIRST ANGEL

*N*ero and I walked down the hall in silence. I didn't bring up our dinner and duel last night. Since I'd already decided that nothing could happen between us, there was really no point. I had a long list of reasons why we could never be together, the top one being that I wouldn't be able to do what I had to do to find Zane if I was mending the inevitable broken heart that a relationship with Nero would end in.

I had reasons—good reasons. Unfortunately, those reasons went right out the window the moment I was alone with him. So I'd just have to make sure to never be alone with him. Our early morning training sessions made that impractical, but I could stay focused for that one hour each morning, right? Other than that, no alone time with Nero. Definitely no visits to his apartment. And when I had to go to his office, I'd remember to leave the door open. Yeah, that was a good plan. What could possibly go wrong?

The skeptic inside of me began to prattle off all the things that would make my brilliant plan crash and burn. I silenced that nasty little voice. I had to think positively. Against all odds, I'd survived the initiation into the Legion and the gods' first gift. That meant I had a strong will. Compared to the trials the Legion threw at me every day, not thinking about Nero should be easy.

"You're unsettled."

I nearly jumped at his words. I covered my unease with a shrug. "Who me? No, I'm fine."

He gave me a hard look, that special one that told me he knew I was full of shit. "You need to learn to lie better. Every breath, every scent, every beat of your heart—it's all a dead giveaway."

"Good to know," I said with a smile that hurt my jaw. "I'll work on it."

"I make you uncomfortable." It wasn't a statement; it was a fact. There was no pity in his words, no triumph, no emotion whatsoever. I couldn't decide if that made me feel better or worse.

"I'm just nervous about the First Angel summoning me," I said. "Do you know what this is about?"

He looked at me, his cold eyes betraying nothing. Ok, fine. He wasn't going to tell me. Not that I was surprised. Angels loved their secrets as much as they loved intimidating people.

Nero led me to an office room I'd never been in before. It was twice as large as his own office. A gargantuan desk stood opposite the door, but besides the antique lamp and glass jar of pens in the corner, there was nothing on it. In fact, the whole room had a feeling of disuse about it. It was just too clean and orderly. It must be the First Angel's office for those times she visited.

Nyx herself stood in the center of the room in all her angelic glory, a beautiful carpet under her feet. Her stance was strong and regal. She wore a glossy black leather suit that accentuated every curve in her body. She was more slender than voluptuous, but that didn't make her presence any less imposing. High-heeled boots added to her already impressive height.

Her eyes, as blue as the ocean, tracked me across the room. She was wearing her glossy black hair long and braided today. The last time I'd seen her, her hair had been chin-length. Either it had grown twenty inches overnight, or she had some seriously powerful magic to be able to shift her appearance like that. That kind of magic was a shifter skill, but most shifters—and Legion soldiers who'd gained the ability—just changed into an animal or maybe two. I'd never seen someone shift only their hair to make it grow.

Nyx was powerful, more powerful than even Nero. I could feel her magic crackling the air, popping against my skin like an electric storm. It was no surprise that she was the First Angel. She felt like a god. Not that I'd ever been in the presence of a god, but this was exactly how I'd always imagined they would feel like. The sheer power inside of Nyx was making the hair on my arms stand up like I'd been zapped by lightning. She'd been holding back her magic before, but not this time. This time, she was letting it all out.

Nero dropped to his knees in recognition of her power, and I did the same. If you were in the presence of the First Angel when she let out her magic, you didn't salute; you bowed. Nyx watched us, her face almost curious as her eyes fell on me. I dropped my gaze quickly from her eyes.

"Rise, Colonel Windstriker."

Nero did as she bade him, but his gaze darted to me, as though afraid I'd offend the First Angel by rising before I was commanded to do so. He needn't have worried. I knew better than to provoke an angel. Well, at least most of the time.

Nyx looked down at me. "You have very unusual hair."

I'd heard that so many times before. Too many times. Vampires especially liked my hair. It was a magnet for them, a beacon that invited them to abandon reason and try to take a nip at me. And I had no idea why. Besides my hair being so pale it was nearly white, there wasn't anything unusual about it that I could see.

Even though it was annoying to hear about my weird hair for the millionth time, I kept my head low and said, "Yes, First Angel."

"You may call me Your Holiness."

I didn't dare glance up to see if she was smirking as she said it, but I thought I caught a hint of humor in her otherwise earnest tone. Was she serious or making fun of herself? I had a feeling it was a bit of both. What an unusual angel.

Nyx reached down, rubbing my hair between her fingers. "There is magic in it."

I'd guessed that. Just because I couldn't detect it, that didn't mean it wasn't there. After all, vampires had to be attracted to something about it besides its shiny color.

"Yes, First Angel," I said again. "I mean, Your Holiness."

Nyx chuckled softly. "Is she always this compliant, Colonel?"

"If only it were so. You've read my reports."

"Yes, I have." She set her hand on my shoulder. "Rise." I rose out of my knees, and as our eyes met, she nodded. "Yes. You will do."

"For what?" I asked before I could think better of it.

Nero shot me a stern look. He was obviously afraid the First Angel, General of the Legion's Armies, was less forgiving of my impudence than he was.

But Nyx didn't seem to care about my speaking out of turn. "I have a mission for you, Leda Pierce."

This time, I waited for her to speak again, even though I was bursting with curiosity.

"Colonel Windstriker has prepared a mission to covertly infiltrate the New York University of Witchcraft so that we may investigate whether they had anything to do with the poisoning yesterday," she said. "For the past few months, two of New York's largest witch covens have been on the brink of open hostilities. The heads of both covens have a seat on the university's board. Obviously, the Legion wants to prevent a war, as that would destabilize the entire city. So we're sending a team to mediate the dispute before it gets out of hand. Colonel Windstriker will lead the team. He has selected Captain Somerset to assist him in the mediation. She is a skilled interrogator." Nyx nodded in approval. "He has provided me with a list of his support team. Do you know who is on that list?"

"No," I said, though I was starting to get a pretty good idea. Nero would have seen this mission as good training for me.

"Not you," Nyx told me.

I looked at Nero in surprise.

"He selected Jace Fireswift and Mira Ravenfall," Nyx said. "Both come from distinguished families that have served the Legion since its early years. Both have an angel parent."

Yeah, the brats were just awesome. "So if I'm not going on the mission, why am I here?" I asked her, checking my annoyance.

"Who said you weren't going on the mission?" she said, smiling. "I merely said you aren't on Colonel Windstriker's list. You are, however, at the top of mine. I've read his reports about you, how you went after him on the Black Plains, how it was you who uncovered that the demons were behind the illegal turning of vampires. You are brave and resourceful. You know how to adapt to a situation, rather than just following patterns you've been taught. That makes you perfect for this mission. You will need to adapt and stay on your toes. I need someone who can think for herself to solve problems without any handholding. Do you think you can do that?"

"I've never been much of a hand-holder," I told her.

Nero was giving me his signature look: an expressionless mask hiding a storm of expressions. I ignored him and kept my attention on the First Angel.

"Calm down, Colonel," Nyx said, her mouth twisting with amusement. "I'm not going to execute your favorite student with my holy arsenal of Earth-shattering magic."

I decided right then and there that I liked Nyx. She was cool. Past her angel feathers and Legion uniform and regal beauty, she seemed like someone who didn't take herself as seriously as someone in her position should. She seemed so… human. It was funny to think of an angel as human, especially the First Angel, but Nyx was exactly that. It gave me hope that you didn't have to sacrifice your humanity to earn your wings.

"I do wonder why she's not on your list, though," Nyx continued, arching her brows at Nero.

"She's not ready," he said simply.

"I think you'd be surprised." Nyx looked at me. "Do you think you're ready for this?"

"Yes," I told her, not looking at Nero as I said it.

"There you have it, Colonel." She shot him a look that was almost impish, then she turned to me. "You will leave for the university the day after tomorrow as part of Colonel Windstriker's team. While the others are interrogating the staff and students about the rift in the witch community, you are to investigate on campus to ascertain how the witches' Sunset Pollen and Snapdragon Venom ended up in a poison that killed nearly a hundred people yesterday at the Brick Palace. Colonel Windstriker will provide you with maps and background on the school. I expect regular reports of your progress." She walked past us like a gust of fresh air, turning just before she left the room to say to me, "Congratulations on the promotion."

What did that mean? But before I could ask her, she was gone, the faint, sweet aroma of peaches in the air the only evidence that she'd ever been here. Nero walked to the door and shut it, then he just stared at me.

I grasped for a diversion and found only sass. It would have to do. "Don't give me that look, Nero. It's not my fault she picked someone not on your list. Why didn't you put me on the list, by the way?"

"As I said, you're not ready," he replied coolly.

"I can do this. I can investigate. I did these kinds of things back in my old bounty-hunting days." I smirked at him. "I am a first rate snoop."

"Which is why Nyx wants you on the team," he said. "But this is far more dangerous than anything you've faced before. And it's too early."

"The First Angel doesn't think it's too early."

"Nyx put you on my team because she believes you can think for yourself and because you are scrappy."

I grinned. "So basically all those things you don't like about me."

"I do like you. Too much for our own good."

His hand flashed out, catching mine. As his thumb began to trace small circles across my palm, my inner voice screamed out in panic, but I didn't move. And I didn't have to. He dropped my hand and took a step back. I tried not to feel too disappointed.

"This is dangerous," he said.

"Aw, you're worried about me," I teased. "I promise not to pick a fight with those witches so they have no reason to throw their calculators at me."

"This is serious, Leda. Witches aren't to be taken lightly. Especially if they're working with the demons."

"Do you really think the demons are behind this?"

"It's a distinct possibility. They did turn witches to their side before. Some of those turned witches might still be at the school, working there or studying as students."

"I'll be careful," I promised him.

"It's not just the witches." He moved to the cabinet behind the desk and opened a drawer. "There is a challenge you must face first." He set an antique glass bottle down on the table.

"Is that…"

"Yes," he said. "The gods' second gift, Witch's Cauldron."

That's what Nyx had meant by the promotion. *Level two, here I come.*

"Tomorrow evening, we will have the ceremony. Prepare yourself."

I almost laughed. How was I supposed to prepare myself for that? At about this time tomorrow, I would drink from the Nectar of the gods once more. And then I would either be granted the second power of the Legion—or be granted an early grave.

"Get some rest, Pandora," he told me. "You'll need it."

Thus dismissed, I left her office, but I didn't go straight back to my dorm room. I took the long way down the corridor, using the time to settle the nervousness bubbling inside of me. Sure, I'd said I was ready, but I hadn't realized I'd have to survive another ceremony first.

But this is exactly what you wanted, said a voice inside of me. *You need to gain more magic so you can find Zane.*

The rational part of me knew that voice was right. This was exactly what I needed. But the dark, terrified part of me wouldn't listen to reason. It kept flashing images of my own death through my head. And if I died, who would save Zane? Only someone who loved him could link to him from so far away. That's how that kind of magic worked. If I didn't make it, that left Calli and my sisters. And the only way they could gain this magic was by joining the Legion too.

No! I clenched my fists, my fear hardening into determination. I would not let them risk their lives. It was up to me to do this. I would survive, and I would save Zane. There wasn't any other way.

With that settled, I headed back toward my room. I didn't make it far. A lieutenant I didn't know ran past me, then he just stopped.

"Don't stand there gawking," he said. "Hurry. We need to contain the situation."

I ran alongside him. "What situation? What's going on?"

Screams and the roar of gunfire echoed down the hall, answering my question. The Legion was under attack.

CHAPTER 7

*I*t wasn't an attack; it was a massacre. When the lieutenant and I burst into the ballroom, it took a moment for me to make sense of the crowd of frightened people cowered before a line of Legion soldiers—and then I remembered what day it was. Today was the first of October. Every two months, on the first of the month, the Legion held an initiation ceremony open to anyone brave or desperate enough to risk their life for a chance to join our ranks. Two months ago, I'd been one of the people standing there, watching people die as I wondered if I would survive the night.

Except this time was worse, so much worse. Dead bodies littered the floor, and it wasn't just the Nectar that had killed them. Half of them had died from gunshot wounds. The initiates must have panicked when the Nectar had started killing the people in front of them in line. They were holding back now, more afraid of the certain bullet to the head than of the fifty percent chance of their body overloading from the Nectar. They weren't running, but they weren't still either. Their bodies twitched, and fear rolled off of them in nauseating waves. Frozen, I stood there and watched, trying to contain the horror tearing through me. Every fiber of humanity in me screamed in desperate protest at the inhumanity of it all.

Past the wall of leather and steel and magic, past the crowd of terrified strangers, Nero stood beside a fountain of gurgling crimson liquid. His wings were out, glowing with a heavenly beauty that seemed to mock the fear hanging heavy in the room. His skin glowed too, flushed with magic, but his eyes were as cold and hard as green diamonds.

One-by-one, the initiates marched up to him and drank from the goblet. When it was all done, only thirteen had survived. They followed Captain Somerset out of the ballroom. I could do nothing but stare at their terrified faces, wondering if their expression was mirrored on my own. That horrible scene was certainly seared into my mind. My heart ached for the dead, and it ached for the survivors. My initiation ceremony hadn't been pretty, but it hadn't been…this. Half of our numbers hadn't been massacred by Legion soldiers—people the new initiates now had to work and live beside every day until death claimed them.

I looked around the ballroom for Ivy or Drake, but they weren't here. I didn't know if I was glad that they didn't have to see this or depressed that I didn't have a shoulder to cry on. My friends must have been moving our things upstairs, I realized.

My memories all clicked into place. Oh, that's right. Last week, the Legion had informed everyone in my initiation group that we were all getting a room upgrade on the first of the month. Ivy, Drake, and I now had a three-bedroom apartment. Between the situation with the witches and everything else that was going on right now, I'd been too distracted to think about my changing living arrangements.

Where I slept seemed so irrelevant in the grand scheme of things.

I stared across the room, finding Nero immediately, but when he turned toward me, I looked away. I couldn't talk to him right now, not after the cold way he'd watched all of those initiates get shot or poisoned to death.

Soldiers were carrying off the dead initiates. They didn't look troubled by all the death. They'd undoubtably seen it all so many times before that they'd hardened their souls. I knew I was expected to do the same, to close off everything that made me human, but I just couldn't. All those bodies, all that innocence—gone. Someone had to mourn for them. My eyes burned with unshed tears, and my mind choked on the finality of their deaths.

Acid singed my throat. I pushed blindly past the soldiers carrying the bodies and ran straight for the bathroom. I barged into the nearest stall and bent over the toilet to throw up everything in my stomach. Even when there was nothing left, my body heaved and quaked. My legs gave out, and I collapsed to the cold floor, shivering.

"Leda."

I didn't turn at the sound of Nero's voice. "Go away."

Instead, he lowered to his knees and lifted me into his arms. As he carried me out of the stall, I pushed against his hold, but I was too weak right now to stand a chance.

"Please," I croaked, the word scraping against my throat like sandpaper. "Leave me alone." I turned my face away from him, hiding my tears.

I was surprised when he didn't carry me into the hallway. Instead, he lowered me to the floor across from the sink. We sat there in silence on the icy marble floor, side by side, our backs pressed against the wall.

"You reacted strongly," he finally said.

I turned my head to meet his cool stare. "And you didn't react at all. How can you be so cold? How can you act like all that death doesn't bother you?"

"I've learned to shut off that part of me."

"Well, I haven't."

"I know." He folded his hands together on top of his raised knees. "Why did you come to the ballroom tonight?"

"I didn't mean to. There was this lieutenant. He ran past me in the hallway and told me to come with him. I thought we were being attacked. I'd forgotten what day it was."

"I didn't want you to see that."

"Those people." I brushed a tear from my eye. "They were so scared. Couldn't you have calmed them?"

"You mean use my magic to control them?"

"Yes."

"I could have calmed them," he said. "But that wouldn't do them any favors. Soldiers of the Legion must be strong. They must face their fears and rise above them. Calming them with magic might have put off their deaths for a few weeks, but it would not have saved them in the end. Their will was not strong enough to survive the Legion."

"That is a very callous attitude," I told him.

"It is the way of life at the Legion. Sometimes, the initiates are strong and sometimes not. Most of the initiates in this group were not."

"Is it often that bad?" I asked.

"No, but it is never pretty. Your ceremony was among our less violent ones."

"It didn't feel that way at the time."

"I know." He reached out to touch my shoulder, but he withdrew his hand, as though he'd thought better of it. "I wish…" He sighed. "I wish you'd gone back to your room like I asked you to. I wanted you as far away from this as possible."

"Why?"

"Because I knew exactly how you would react," he said. "I knew it would hurt you to see it. You are too good for this."

"I thought I had a good side and a bad side."

"Not a good side and a bad side. A light side and a dark side," he corrected me. "It's different. You have both darkness and light, but you are all good. You're compassionate. And you fight fiercely for those you love. You're tough, Leda, but that toughness doesn't cover your heart. It hurt you to watch those people die, even though you do not know them."

I leaned my head against his shoulder. "You don't mind?" I glanced up at him. "I know it's not appropriate. But just for a little bit…"

He wrapped his arm around my shoulder, pulling me tightly against him. We must have looked ridiculous sitting here on the bathroom floor, but right now I wouldn't have been anywhere else. You didn't mourn the passing of innocent souls in a warm, comfortable bathtub full of bubbles. That just wouldn't be right.

"Thank you," I whispered to Nero as the tears rolled down my cheeks.

He didn't say anything, and I found it didn't matter. The fact that he was here was enough. I cried until my eyes were dry and the hurt in my heart was starting to dull. He sat beside me the whole time, his arm wrapped around my shoulder.

"Nero?"

He glanced down at me. "Yes?"

"I don't want to get used to this," I said. "I don't want to grow cold to it. I don't want icicles to freeze over my heart."

"You don't have a single icicle in you, Leda Pierce," he told me. "Feeling is as natural to you as breathing. And I don't believe you will ever lose your humanity. Not like some of us."

"Nero, you're more human than you know." I reached up to my shoulder and squeezed the hand he'd wrapped around it.

"I can't afford to be human," he said, pulling away.

I held to him. "Just another moment, Colonel."

He could have broken free of me. He certainly was strong enough. And yet he stayed with me. I wasn't sure if he was doing it out of pity or out of a sense of obligation, and I didn't really care. Even as I intertwined my fingers with his, he didn't pull away. He kept on holding me. My chest quivering with sadness, I dropped my head to his shoulder and mourned for the people who had died tonight, for those who'd died yesterday, and for every person who would die before this was all over.

I welcomed the training exercises the next day. I pushed myself harder than ever before, and for a time, that was enough to bury thoughts of last night's ballroom massacre. But as I stood in my new apartment at the end of the day, my hands began to shake—and it wasn't just from exhaustion.

"Are you all right?" Ivy asked me, coming out of her bedroom. "Are you nervous about the ceremony tonight?"

"Yes," I answered, even as images from last night flashed through my head.

Ivy squeezed my hand. "I know you'll make it."

"Thanks." I offered her a half-smile. At the moment, it was the best I could do. Between the sick clenching of my stomach over what had happened last night and my shot nerves anticipating what would happen tonight, I was a mess.

"Just think about something else," Ivy said. "Like how great our new apartment is. Hey, we even have a bathtub." She rubbed her hands together in glee.

Our new apartment was certainly an improvement over our old dormitory, but it was hard not to dwell on the reason for our upgrade: a batch of new initiates had come to the Legion last night and taken our place in the dorms. Terrified screams and gunfire tore with merciless finality through my mind.

No, I couldn't think about that. I had to be strong. Zane was counting on me, and there was no time for a mental breakdown. Ivy was right. I had to think about something else. I focused on our new apartment. It wasn't as glamorous as the apartments on the top floor of the building—those that housed Legion officers level six and up—but Ivy had spruced up the place. Scented candles and jars with incense sticks stood atop lace doilies on every table and shelf in the living room, filling the air with the sweet, welcoming scent of vanilla, lilacs, and roses.

Past the living room, four doors led to the bathroom and three bedrooms. Each bedroom was only large enough to fit a bed, a small nightstand, and a closet. I'd never had my own bedroom before. Rather than being excited about the idea, a feeling of intense loneliness filled me. I missed the old room I shared with my sister Bella back at home. My heart clenched up as I realized that I would never again live under the same roof as Calli and my brother and sisters. The Legion was my life now, but would they ever be my family?

I looked at Ivy, who was zigzagging across the room, humming to herself as she tidied up her decorations. Only a month ago, she'd lost her mother, the person she'd joined the Legion to save, but she was still carrying on. If anything, she was moving faster than ever. Training harder, decorating, dancing, and partying—basically, being constantly on the go —that was how she was dealing with her loss. And she was doing an amazing job of staying upbeat.

"You're awesome, you know," I told her.

"Of course she is," Drake said as he closed the mini

fridge he'd set up in the living room. It was completely filled with tiny alcohol bottles and just-as-tiny juice bottles.

Ivy beamed at us. "Just wait until you see the blankets I'm knitting." She smoothed out the doily that sat under the pale yellow candle on the mini fridge. "And now, Leda, let's get you ready for tonight."

I walked into my room, Ivy right behind me. As soon as I opened my closet, she tossed a scented bundle of potpourri at me.

"For your lingerie drawer," she said with a wink.

"Thanks," I said, sliding open my underwear drawer. "You can't go wrong with floral-scented panties."

"Exactly," she replied, grinning.

"So, I'm headed downstairs to help set up the ballroom for the ceremony," Drake said from my door. His eyes darted from the potpourri bag to the open underwear drawer, a smile curling his mouth. "I never took you for a lace and ribbons sort of girl, Leda."

I blushed. "My sister Tessa thinks I ought to be, so she sent me these things—and convinced my other sisters to do the same."

"Your sister is very wise," Ivy said, her hand flashing out to recover a pair of red panties from my drawer.

"And that's my cue to leave," Drake said, heading for the front door.

"Ok, so what are you thinking?" Ivy asked me when he was gone.

"I'm trying not to."

"Don't be nervous. It will be fine. You will do great. I can't believe you're up for level two already. And, by the way, so is Jace." Her smile faded, and she rolled her eyes.

So Jace was still coming along on Nero's mission, which

meant I'd replaced Mira. If she ever found out about that, she'd have yet another reason to hate my guts.

"But I meant, what are you thinking about wearing tonight?" Ivy asked.

"Uh…well…"

She moved past me. She reached into my closet and pulled out a red leather miniskirt and a black top with larger pieces of material missing from the front and sides. No, the moths hadn't eaten through the fabric. It was intentionally cut out. The top was another gift from Tessa. My seventeen-year-old sister had interesting ideas of what constituted an article of clothing. What she insisted was a top, I called only a piece of a top. Ivy clearly shared Tessa's taste. She nodded and smiled at it in approval before tossing the questionable shirt onto my bed.

"Are you sure about this?" I asked, holding up the leather miniskirt.

"Positive."

"Why? So if I fall, everyone will see my underwear?"

Ivy smirked at me. "Exactly. Hence the red lace panties, of course. They match."

I stripped out of my sports clothes. "I was thinking of just wearing my uniform."

Ivy snorted. "Who are you now, Nero Windstriker? No, trust me, honey. The Legion is wise in letting you pick what you're going to wear for the ceremony. They want you to party, and we're not going to disappoint them."

"Or they're just letting us decide what we'll die in."

"Hey, don't think like that." Ivy squeezed my shoulder. "Everything will be fine."

I took a deep breath, inhaling her optimism. "I know." Last night had been a harrowing reminder of how dangerous life here was, but after what I'd seen, I was even more determined to make it through all of this and find Zane. I didn't want anyone in my family to ever have to join the Legion.

"So tonight is a busy ceremony," Ivy said in her light-hearted tone as I put on the red lingerie. "It's you going for level two. And Jace too." She gave her eyes another long roll. "Then Corporal Lynch and Corporal Solis going for level three. And Lieutenant Diaz going for level six."

"Is this the same Lieutenant Diaz who worships the ground you walk on?" I asked her, sliding the skirt over my hips.

"The one and same," she replied with a gleeful grin.

She was changing into a skin-tight black and white dress that was cut halfway to her knees. She topped off the look with a pair of gold high-heeled shoes. Her red hair was down tonight, falling to her elbows in bouncy curls.

"There will be music and dancing," Ivy said. "And tons of food. It will be great."

I smoothed out my top, then slid into a pair of black leather boots. "Ok, I'm ready."

Ivy's explosion of laughter echoed off my empty walls. "Oh, no you don't. Not so fast. I'm doing your hair and makeup. I am not letting you out of here looking anything short of one hundred percent fantastic."

————

By the time Ivy was through with me, I did look fantastic—if not a bit slutty. That was exactly what she'd been going for, she'd assured me with a wink as we headed downstairs.

Two large standing vases stood on either side of the double doors that led into the ballroom. A scene of angels fighting monsters was painted on each vase, the masterful strokes of color even more beautiful than the giant flowers shooting out of the tops. Past the entrance, beams of golden light shone against the walls, and a web of blue twinkling lights hung overhead like thousands of tiny stars. And beneath that majestic sky, hundreds of Legion soldiers filled the ballroom. It felt like the whole New York office was in attendance. They stood chatting around the buffet tables and bar, and they danced across the floor with supernatural grace. Skirts and tuxedo tails twirled and turned in hypnotic swooshes of light and color.

"We're underdressed," I muttered to Ivy, looking out across the room. Almost everyone was dressed in formal wear. They were decked out in silk and chiffon while we were wearing leather and spandex.

"Nonsense," Ivy laughed, indicating a small group of people dressed just like we were. "Besides, don't you want to stand out?"

No, I didn't want to stand out. I wanted to blend into the shadows. As we headed toward the dance floor, I could feel hundreds of eyes turn toward me, but when I looked, no one was staring. It must have been my imagination. I was letting Nerissa's words get to me. Most of those people didn't even know who I was.

Ivy's admiring lieutenant stepped into our path, bowing deeply before her. She giggled, then took his hand. As the happy couple waltzed their way across the dance floor, I sat down at the bar and ordered myself a pineapple juice. Even though my nerves were shot, I didn't dare order anything harder. I couldn't take any chances of the alcohol reacting badly to the heavy dose of Nectar I was about to ingest.

"She moves pretty well," Captain Somerset said, sitting down beside me. Her dark eyes followed Ivy and her partner's smooth sequence of steps. "Considering how she's dressed."

I turned to look at Captain Somerset, who was wearing the most feminine outfit I'd ever seen on her: a sleeveless pink-and-white ballgown with a full chiffon skirt. Her dark hair was pulled back into a high twist, and chandelier earrings hung from her ears.

"Are you wearing makeup?" I asked her in shock, reminding myself not to stare.

"I wear makeup all the time."

I arched my brows at her.

She chuckled. "Ok, I wear makeup when there's an official Legion function to attend."

"It looks good."

"Don't be a smart ass." Still grinning, she looked me up and down. "Nice outfit." She tossed a piece of popcorn into her mouth.

"It was Ivy's idea."

She cast a longer look down the length of my body. "Good choice. It shows off your ass and your boobs. Nero will like it."

I opened my mouth to say something, but nothing came out. I popped it shut again, my face scorching. I wished I could just melt into the floor. I was hit with the feeling again that everyone was watching me, and this time when I turned, I saw I was right.

"They all like your outfit too," Captain Somerset said, her gaze trailing mine around the room.

"Or they're just gossiping about me," I muttered.

"Of course they are. You've only been at the Legion for two months, and already you're up for a promotion. People aren't usually that fast. Ok, Nero was, but he's special."

"And freakishly, frighteningly powerful."

"That too," she agreed.

"Well, Jace is up for the second level too, and no one is staring at him."

"He is the son of an angel," she said, shrugging.

I sighed. "True."

"You must also remember that the Legion is like no other military on Earth. Magical potential can make you move fast and far, and the children of angels have a lot of potential. The gods need powerful soldiers for their army. They want each of us to reach our full potential, to have as much magic as we can handle because that makes the Legion itself stronger. It's a balance between making sure we don't die and pushing us as high as we can go."

"Do people die at the higher levels?" I asked her.

"Sometimes," she said. "But rarely. The Legion makes sure you're ready before pushing you to the next level. Nero wouldn't have you do this if he weren't sure you were ready."

Except Nero didn't want me to do this. He didn't think I was ready. This was all Nyx's doing, and she didn't know me at all. Maybe Nero was right. Maybe I wasn't ready. I couldn't tell Captain Somerset that, though.

So I said, "Well, I suppose there are worse things people could be staring at me about."

"Oh, you mean like how they're wondering when you and Nero will sleep together?" Her whole face lit up. "Yeah, they're watching you because of that too."

I ground my teeth together.

She chuckled lightly. "It's a hard, hard life at the Legion. Give the poor people something to gossip about."

"Says the person not under their microscope."

"Oh, I've been under their microscope myself," she said. "Angels' love lives are always a cause for gossip at the Legion, and I was once involved with one."

"How long did it last?"

A dreamy look slid across her face. "Not long enough. As I once told you, angels make great lovers. Though they can be a moody bunch."

I glanced across the room at Nero, who was standing beside Nyx, talking to her. He was the only person in the entire ballroom wearing a uniform. Not that it didn't look good on him… But he just looked so serious.

"A moody bunch, you say? I never could have guessed," I said drily.

"Well, it's an on-and-off sort of thing," Captain Somerset told me. "But when it's on, it's *on*. You'll know what I mean soon enough."

Nero had finished his conversation with Nyx, and he was walking alongside the dance floor, his emerald eyes pulsing with power as they met mine.

I looked away. "I don't know why everyone is so certain that Nero and I are going to get together," I told Captain Somerset.

She snorted. "Are you kidding? There's so much heat between you two that I'm getting a sunburn just being in the same room with you."

Nero was nearly to the bar.

"I don't think I'm comfortable talking about this with you," I said to her.

"You're right," she said, smiling with a sweetness that had me worried. "You shouldn't be talking to me. Just skip straight to dessert." Then she gave me a hard push that sent me tumbling off my stool and right into Nero.

He caught me easily, steadying my fall. "Yes?" he asked me as Captain Somerset melted into the crowd.

"I…" I cleared my throat. "Captain Somerset pushed me into you."

"I see."

85

I tried to read something in his face, but as usual, he'd put up a wall of cool marble that would take a bulldozer to smash through.

"Thank you," I said awkwardly. "For last night. For being there."

He inclined his chin but said nothing. Wow, this sure was fun. I'd had more exciting conversations with myself. Well, what was I expecting anyway? The guy was the only one here who'd worn a uniform to the party. Even Nyx, the First Angel of the Legion, was wearing a long satin gown.

"So." I put on a smile. "How have you been?"

"Busy." His gazed darted across the room. "I have to go."

"Oh, ok." I tried not to sound disappointed—which I most certainly was *not*.

Yeah, you just keep telling yourself that, said the voice of doubt in my head.

Nero walked away, leaving me alone and feeling stupid. Wow, I was a master orator tonight. Why weren't the words coming out right? Why was my tongue tripping over every other syllable? I needed to be witty and interesting, but I was just dull and uninspiring. What had happened between us was throwing me for a loop. He'd comforted me in my moment of turmoil, and now things were…weird. I wasn't really sure what to say to him anymore. Not that I should be worrying about this. I'd already decided that Nero and I weren't going to be anything.

With that cleared up, I turned to look for Ivy, but she was dancing with Drake now. I didn't want to interrupt that. On the other side of the dance floor, beside the cupcake tower, Nerissa and Captain Somerset were chatting. Now *that* was a dangerous conversation. I couldn't imagine what the unfiltered queens of the Legion were talking about—and I was sure I didn't want to know.

I was about to go talk to my former dormitory roommate Lucy when the music stopped and the golden ceiling lights brightened. All eyes turned to the brightest spot in the room, a raised platform. Nero stood there, in front of a table that held three antique colored bottles, each one about the size of a wine bottle. And beside those three bottles were three goblets.

"Welcome," Nero said, his voice carrying across the whole ballroom, filling it so that it seemed he was speaking from every direction. "We bear witness here today as five of our own challenge themselves once more to take their next step in life, to strengthen themselves and the Legion in preparation for the days to come."

"For the days to come," everyone repeated around me.

"Soren Diaz, step forward," Nero said.

The crowd parted, and Ivy's admirer walked toward the stage. He moved with a strong, supple gait—his body and his mind both hardened by the Legion's merciless training regimen. His steps were steady and his head held high, but I could feel a subtle flutter of anxiety wafting off of him. No one else showed any sign of noticing. Or they were simply all too professional to show that they had.

He stopped before Nero. Eyes nearly as dark as his black hair met the angel's green stare. Nero took a bottle from the table and began to fill one of the goblets. A pale gold liquid that looked like yellow milk gurgled out.

"Sip now of the gods' Nectar," Nero recited, handing him the full goblet. "Consume the magic of their sixth gift. Let it fill you, making you strong for the days to come."

"For the days to come," everyone repeated again. The words must be some kind of Legion catchphrase, but I'd never heard them before.

Lieutenant Diaz drank. As he did, his face contorted in

agony, but he didn't stop drinking, not even for a second. When the goblet was empty, he set it down on the table. Then, suddenly, he stumbled to the side, throwing out a hand to catch himself on the wall. His body shook and pain streamed down his face, but he remained on his feet with the unyielding stubbornness that defined the Legion. After a few shaky moments, he managed to straighten. He met Nero's eyes once more. Nero nodded, and Lieutenant Diaz turned and stepped off the platform, disappearing into the crowd.

Then Nero called out once more in a voice that seemed to hit me from every direction, "Cassia Lynch, step forward."

A short woman with a long black braid walked up to the platform, the train of her long periwinkle-blue chiffon gown slithering across the floor after her as she moved. Nero poured from the second bottle into a different goblet. This dose of Nectar was amber-colored, resembling maple syrup.

"Sip now of the gods' Nectar," said Nero. "Consume the magic of their third gift. Let it fill you, making you strong for the days to come."

"For the days to come," everyone repeated.

Corporal Lynch took the goblet into her hands and drank long and deep. She held herself together well, keeping her face neutral even as her chest shook with internal convulsions. She just stood there, immovable, waiting. Finally, her body stopped twitching, and Nero dismissed her.

Next came Corporal Solis, also up for the third level. He wore a suave tuxedo and black shoes that shone like pure oil, but his charming exterior cracked when he almost threw up the Nectar he'd received. He managed to hold himself together—and the Nectar down. Nero dismissed him as well.

After him came Jace. He threw back the entire contents of the goblet in a single go. He looked less sick than the last guy, but he was definitely shaken. As soon as Nero was satisfied he wouldn't die, he dismissed him. Jace walked away, his steps wobbling.

And then it was my turn.

"Leda Pierce, step forward."

All eyes turned from Nero to me. Whispers sizzled up on the crowd, though they'd been silent during the ceremonies before mine.

"Be silent," Nero said, his voice cutting like a whip through their whispers. The chatting died in an instant.

I walked forward, the hard heels of my boots snapping with false confidence against the smooth floor. My eyes remained locked on the target: the goblet Nero had just filled with a bright pink fluid. Turmoil twisted inside of my stomach, filling me with dread.

A month ago, I watched in horror as six of my fellow initiates died after sipping the Nectar of the gods, a heavenly drink that either grants you magical powers or kills you. I can't believe I'm coming back for seconds.

"Sip now of the gods' Nectar. Consume the magic of their second gift." Nero's eyes bored into mine. "Let it fill you, making you strong for the days to come."

"For the days to come," everyone repeated.

The goblet shook in my hands. Nearby, Nyx was watching me with an intensity that was almost blinding.

"This will give you the power of Witch's Cauldron. You will need it to wield the witches' power over potions and brews," Nero whispered to me.

My heart stuttered when he handed me the goblet, and not just because I was scared of dying from that dose. The way he was looking at me scared me at least as much.

"You are strong," he said in that same low whisper.

"I thought I wasn't ready," I whispered back with a smile.

"*I* am not ready. There's always a chance…"

"As I told you so many times before, I'm too stubborn to die," I said with a confidence that I didn't feel—but I hoped would infect me, driving out my anxiety. Holding his stare, I took a deep breath, swallowing my fears, and then I drank.

The Nectar washed through me, igniting my magic. An exotic flavor exploded on my tongue, one that I couldn't define but reminded me of Nero's blood. I glanced at him, and before I knew what I was doing, my tongue flicked out to lick my lips. My whole body was alive, buzzing, singing from the high of the Nectar. Magic cascaded through me in dizzying, euphoric waves that left my mouth dry and my body pounding with an ache that was as bitter as it was sweet. A fresh rush of power knocked me off balance. Nero's hands flashed out, catching me. A collective gasp of shock buzzed across our audience.

"Are you all right?" he asked quietly.

I steadied myself. "Fine," I said, wetting my lips.

If I'd said anything else, I would have slurred my way through the words. I was feeling so drunk. The room was spinning like a carousel of lights and magic. I laughed, and our audience's gasps elevated into rapid streams of shocked whispers. Nyx was at the forefront of the crowd, her arms at her sides in a balletic pose, her face impassive.

As I stood there, reveling in the Nectar's magic, I felt like every cell in my body had been jolted awake. I was hyper-aware of everything. The cool breeze coming in from the windows. The scent of flowers and sugar in the air. How close Nero was to me. I caught myself as I leaned in toward him. Through the haze of my mind, a voice was telling me that kissing Nero in front of the Legion's entire New York office wasn't a good idea. So I pivoted around and tried my best to disappear back into the crowd.

"The gods have tested your fortitude and judged you worthy," Nero said to us.

A waltz started up over the speakers, the lights around the platform dimmed, and people started dancing again—much to my chagrin as I was currently standing in the middle of the dance floor. I moved around the turning couples, my steps drunken, my mind buzzing. Why was my reaction to the Nectar so different from everyone else's? The Nectar made every other person sick, but it only made me want more. Sure, the small Nectar drops the Legion soldiers drank at parties got them high and happy, but those drops were totally diluted compared to this Nectar. This Nectar cranked up your magic, giving you the gods' next magical gift—or it killed you. It did not leave you drunk and craving more.

Buzzing off the Nectar, I sashayed over to the bar and ordered a pineapple cocktail sans alcohol. As the bartender handed me my drink, Jace came up to the bar. His black tux sparkled with hundreds of tiny blue dots from the twinkling web of lights overhead.

I waved at him and squinting, said, "Are you wearing two bowties?"

His eyes dipped to my drink. "Are you sure you want to drink that?"

"Why?"

His brows lifted.

"Oh, I get it. Don't worry." I leaned in, whispering, "It's a virgin." I snorted.

"You get drunk on Nectar," Jace said calmly.

A quiet, distant voice inside of me reminded me that I shouldn't be advertising my weaknesses, especially not to my enemies. But I just couldn't stop laughing. I was still laughing as Ivy and Drake joined us at the bar. Ivy grabbed my arm, pulling me away with them.

"What are you doing talking to *him*?" she hissed under her breath as we walked away.

I blinked. "I'm drunk."

She laughed. "You think?"

"Leda, maybe eating something will kick your metabolize into high gear and help you burn off that high," Drake suggested.

"Great idea," I said brightly, breaking away to launch my assault on the dessert table. I found brownies. Lots and lots of brownies. And I intended to eat every single one of them.

"Hungry?"

I turned to look into Captain Somerset's face. "They're just so good." I licked a brownie crumb from my index finger.

She laughed.

"You're cool," I told her, laughing too.

"You bet I am."

That famous song about the witch who'd fallen for a vampire blared over the fading beat of the waltz.

"Oh, I love this song. It's so funny," I said, looking around. Ivy and Drake were nowhere in sight, so I grabbed Captain Somerset's hand and pulled her onto the dance floor after me.

She didn't seem to mind. In fact, she looked amused as I began to dance to the beat. She danced opposite me, her grin persisting into the second verse. That's when a hand closed around my arm, pulling me roughly around.

"Hey!" My protest died on my lips when I saw that rough someone was Nero—and that he was looking at me with eyes that burned with fury.

"Come with me," he said with a coldness that countered

the heat in his eyes.

"Go easy on her, Nero," Captain Somerset said. "She's wound up right now."

"Thank you, Captain. That will be all," he said to her with equal coldness, but his eyes never left mine.

Captain Somerset turned and walked away, leaving us alone. I looked at Nero, a smile tugging on my mouth.

"I hope I didn't do anything inappropriate," I said, bursting into giggles.

Nero said nothing. His hand still firmly locked around my arm, he led me from the ballroom. I could see people turning to watch us leave, but I couldn't seem to care. Cool. This whole euphoria thing had its perks. It sure beat worrying about what everyone was saying about me. I started laughing. Or maybe I'd never stopped. I couldn't remember. Nero showed me into his office, then closed the door behind us.

"Are you all right?" he asked, finally letting go of my arm.

Closing the door was overkill. It's not like I was planning on running out. Why would I want to be anywhere else right now? I couldn't stop laughing.

"Leda?"

"I like the sound of my name on your tongue." I winked at Nero. "But you can call me Pandora if you want. I like that too." Smiling, I traced my finger across his chest, following the smooth, hard lines of leather. "The bringer of chaos. Of mischief." I allowed my hand to venture lower.

That boring, rational part of me was screaming at me to stop, reminding me of what would happen if I became Nero's lover, but I just couldn't stop. He'd been so sweet to me last night. So tender. And yet so strong. I slid my hand around him, scraping my fingernails into the hard muscle beneath the leather.

I knew the Nectar was making me act like this, but I didn't care. I wanted Nero and he wanted me. There was no reason not to take what I wanted. I leaned back against his desk, arching my back to push out my breasts. His eyes dipped to them, then quickly flickered back to my face.

"You're tempting me," he said, his voice a low, sexy rumble in his chest.

"You tempt me every moment of every day you're in the same room with me. Seeing you there, so close and yet not touching me. It's agonizing, Nero."

A rare look of shock crossed his face. "When the Nectar wears off, you're going to hate yourself for saying that."

"The only person I'm going to hate is you, Nero, if you don't come over this instant and make love to me."

His eyes widened as I dipped my hand below my skirt, slipping my panties down my legs. I kicked them the rest of the way off, and they landed at his feet. Then I hopped onto his desk, hiking up my short skirt.

I saw it the moment I had him. Magic flashed in his eyes, and then the next moment he was suddenly in front of me, his hands pinning mine to the desk. As the heat of his skin burned into me—saturating me—a hollow, wanton ache echoed inside of me, an ache I knew only he could quell.

"I knew," I whispered against his ear. "I knew from the beginning that we would end up like this."

My head fell back, a soft moan escaping my lips as his mouth closed on my neck. His tongue flicked out. The touch of it on my throat shot a shock wave of pure pleasure through me, scorching me from the inside out. His hands closed tightly around my wrists, and my pulse popped against my skin, throbbing in sweet anticipation.

That sweetness turned to ash when he suddenly pulled away. I moved to follow him, but I found myself stuck in place. My gaze dropped to my hands, which were handcuffed to the desk. I pulled against the restraints, but they were Legion-issued and not breakable by someone of my strength.

"What are you doing?" I growled, continuing to push against the cold, unyielding metal around my wrists. "I never expected you were into the kinky stuff."

"You don't know me," he said in a harsh whisper, bracing his hands against his desk as he leaned in. "So don't presume that you know what I'm into." His words slid across my skin like satin promises. His face was so close, and his body so far away.

"Then show me," I said, arching my body toward him.

He pulled away. "This is not you, Leda. It's the Nectar. It should burn through your system, settling in half an hour. When it has, you will be able to see clearly enough to get out of those restraints."

I pounded hard against the restraints, but like Nero, they didn't yield. A strangled stream of curses spilled out of my mouth. His brows lifted, but he didn't say a thing.

"You cruel, twisted angel," I growled as he walked toward the door. "How could you leave me like this?"

A smile touched his lips. He turned back around, and in a flash, his face was in front of mine. "Once the magic has settled inside of you, and you're thinking straight, come see me. I have some work for you to do pre-mission." Each hot caress of his breath against my skin was pure agony. "I will not take advantage of you in this state, but if you still need me after the haze has passed, I would be more than happy to oblige." He kissed my jaw with excruciating, maddening slowness.

And then he was just gone. He left me in his office, chained to his desk. I wasn't sure how long I raged and pushed and kicked, but at some point in all that madness, my head did begin to clear. Sanity returned, bringing with it a most unwelcome guest: shame. My body burned, and it wasn't from desire this time. Mortified, I looked around the room, rocking slowly as I tried not to watch the memory replay looping inside of my head. About this time, Ivy and Drake walked through the open door, their eyes wide.

"Wow," Drake said, laughter overcoming his shock. "When we noticed you were gone, we went looking for you. We heard your curses all the way down the hall. We definitely didn't expect this." His eyes flickered to my handcuffed hands.

My eyes dropped too—and that's when I noticed the series of releases on the handcuffs. Why hadn't I seen that earlier? Oh, because I'd been crazy with Nectar-induced lust, that's why.

"What happened here?" Ivy asked as I freed my hands.

"It isn't what it looks like," I said quickly, jumping off the desk.

She held up my panties, her lips trembling with barely-contained laughter. "Oh really? Because it looks to me like it was a good thing you wore the lacy red panties."

The fire in my cheeks could have forged steel, but my embarrassment was nothing compared to my rage. I was angry at Nero. And at myself. And at the stupid Nectar. Why did I have to have such a strong reaction to it?

"Left you high and dry, did he?" she asked, giving my shoulder a sympathetic pat.

High but not dry. I snatched my underwear from her hand. It was time to put on my big girl panties. I stormed toward the door.

"Where are you going?" Ivy asked.

"I'm going to give that angel a piece of my mind," I told her.

CHAPTER 9

A FOUNDATION OF WITCHCRAFT

*F*ury carried me up the hundreds of stairs to Nero's floor—fury and the sugar rush from all those brownies I'd snarfed down. I marched down the corridor and banged on Nero's door. And then I waited.

None of the doors on the floor opened, even though my knock had been loud enough to wake the dead. Everyone must have still been at the party downstairs. At least I hoped they were. What I was about to do was madness. You didn't just run up to an angel and… And what? What was I going to do?

Before I could contemplate that unhappy dilemma further, Nero's door opened. As soon as I saw him standing there, as soon as I looked into those cool assessing eyes, my anger melted into embarrassment. I remembered everything I'd said in his office—and, worse yet, done. Dear gods, this wasn't good. Maybe if I pretended nothing had happened, this whole thing would just go away.

"I'm ready. Uh, for work," I added quickly in case he thought I was talking about something else. "To receive my mission work." Not to receive him. Oh shit. This wasn't going well.

Amusement flickered across his face before it was swallowed by the cool abyss. "Come in."

"Can't I stay out here?"

"I have a few things to give you. Now stop hugging my doorframe and come inside."

I followed him inside his apartment. He waved his hand at the door, and it closed with a definitive click behind me. Nero was already walking toward his dining room table. There was no food or wine waiting on it tonight, just a stack of papers.

"Here are the blueprints of the five buildings that make up the New York University of Witchcraft," he said, handing me the first bundle of papers. "Memorize the layouts. While the rest of us are in session in the assembly hall, you will look for any evidence of the witches' involvement in the attack on the Brick Palace two days ago. To accomplish that, you'll need to navigate the school quickly and methodically."

I took the folder without a word. Not talking was probably the best plan right now. He hadn't yet mentioned what had happened in his office, and as the reality of the situation set in, I realized that I didn't want to either.

"I've prepared a reading list for you," he said, handing me a list of books ten pages long. Front and back. "You will find these titles in the Legion library on the fourth floor. They should give you a good foundation in witchcraft. You will need that in your investigation."

I could only gawk at the list. Could that many books even fit inside of a single library?

"Now that you have received the gods' second gift, you have the ability to put magic into potions," he said in response to my very attractive deer-in-headlights expression. "You can do anything a witch can."

"I don't feel very witchy."

"It will come."

"So it's just like the last time? I just have to push my way through it until I get it?"

"Basically, yes," he said. "Though mastering Witch's Cauldron is a mental battle, not a physical one like Vampire's Kiss."

Mental battle, right. I could do that. I could be brainy.

That confidence lasted about two seconds, crashing and burning when Nero handed me a second list. "Here is some extra reading material if you get through the first list."

I mutely took it from him. I might be able to finish reading all those books if I did nothing else for the next twenty years. Who needed sleep anyway? It was totally over-rated—kind of like having free time.

"It might be difficult in the beginning, but you will find that the longer you keep at it, the easier it becomes for you to absorb the knowledge," he told me. "The gods have given you a powerful gift. You just need to unlock it."

A tortured, strangled noise escaped my lips. "Can't you just give me more pushups?"

"During our regular training sessions, I will quiz you on the material you've read. You will have the opportunity to demonstrate what you've learned while going through your physical exercises."

From the look on his face, he was perfectly serious. Of course he was. Nero was brutally efficient. Why kill two birds with one stone when you could kill ten with a boulder? I hoped his efficiency didn't kill me too.

"But there will be no training session tomorrow morning.

We will leave early for our meeting with the witches," Nero said.

"Is that all?" I asked. Something in his eyes said it wasn't. Was he going to talk about what had happened downstairs?

"Yes, actually, I did want to speak to you about something."

He moved in closer, and I clutched the paper bundles to my chest. They would make a pitiful shield against an angel, and an even worse sword. Well, unless angels' mortal weakness was a paper cut.

"About what?" I asked, backing up.

"There's no reason to feel terrified," he said impatiently. "I'm not going to bite you."

Was it messed up that a part of me was disappointed by that statement?

Yep, my inner cynic told me. *That is really messed up.*

"It's about Harker," he said.

I stopped backing up. "Has he been judged?"

"No, he is still being questioned," Nero said.

"Still? But it's been a whole month!" I protested.

"Yes, but his situation is difficult. I could not tell the High Angels about the dose of pure Nectar he tried to give you. They would want to know why he gave it to you, and they wouldn't hesitate to use any means necessary."

The meaning of his words could not have been more clear. Nor could the look he gave me. "They would torture me."

"Yes." The soft hiss of that single word was as damning as a chorus of accusations.

"So if the High Angels don't know the truth of what happened, what do they think Harker did?" I asked.

"There was only one reason I could give them for taking Harker into custody: his unsanctioned execution of Rose

Crane. He could have taken her into custody during the battle at Sweet Dreams, but he killed her instead. And by doing so, the Legion was robbed of the opportunity to question the mastermind behind the demons' supernatural recruiting scheme in New York."

Disgust rolled over me. "They would have tortured her, Nero. I might not agree with Harker trying to use me to find my brother for whichever god he's working for, but he killed Rose to spare her years of torture. Between death and torture, I know she would have chosen death herself. I don't know why he did it, but it was an act of mercy."

"I know why he did it," Nero said quietly. "Because despite everything he did, Harker still cares about you. He spared Rose to spare you the guilt of knowing that by going after her, you had doomed her to eternal agony."

"I…I don't know what to say about that." No one had ever killed someone for me before, and I was torn between appreciating his mercy and despising his callous disregard for human life.

Nero watched me closely, as if my face held the key to the world's greatest mystery. "Only time will tell how this plays out—and what the High Angels' response will be. Or, I should say, what Nyx's response will be. She heads the High Angels, and she is personally handling Harker's interrogation."

"Will Harker tell them about the Nectar he tried to give me? Or about Zane?" I asked Nero.

"No," he said immediately. He must have thought this through already. "Harker is acting on the orders of a god, one who is scheming without the knowledge of the others. Just as the demons spelled their followers to withstand interrogation, this god would have done the same to Harker."

"Will the god step in and save him?"

"I don't believe so," said Nero. "He is making a power play of his own. So far, none of the other gods know about your brother."

Right. If all the gods knew about Zane, they'd have already arrested me and forced me to take the Nectar to find him. Only someone with a close connection to Zane could mentally link to him without knowing where he was.

"So the god cannot tip his hand by helping Harker now. At least not directly. In the meantime, I've been trying to figure out which god we're dealing with."

"How?" I didn't think Nero planned to barge into one of their meetings and demand to know which of them was pulling Harker's strings.

"I've been talking to Nyx, asking her discreet questions about the gods to figure out which one might be preparing to make a power play against the others. She knows them better than any of us."

"Because she meets with the gods?" I asked.

"Because one of the gods is her lover," he told me.

Oh, wow. Now that was interesting. I'd never heard of any god taking an angel for a lover, but Nyx was clearly not just any angel. There had to be a reason she was the First Angel.

"Does that relationship make her more impartial or less impartial in dealing with Harker?" I asked. "What if her lover is the god Harker made a deal with? Then she might already know what Zane is." I felt the need to do something, to find my brother now and protect him, but I was still so far from the power I needed to do that. And even if I became an angel and gained that power, I would be no match for a god.

"If Nyx knew about your brother, she could easily concoct a reason to take you into custody. You're not exactly an obedient soldier."

"If you're referring to how I went back out on the Black Plains to rescue you—"

"Nyx doesn't even need a reason that big," he said. "But that reminds me that I still haven't come up with a suitable punishment for your misconduct."

"What do you call all that extra evening running you made me do for the last month?"

"Training. Punishments are less pleasant."

I sighed. "Maybe you'll just let it slide?"

He gave me a hard look. "Does that sound like me?"

"No, not really." I smiled at him. "But how about if I cross my heart and hope to die that I will never do it again?"

"Will you swear an actual oath to that effect? An oath bound by blood, not gilded over in teenage girl bubblegum promises."

"Well, I…" I snorted. "Sorry, no. I can't. If you got yourself captured today, I would totally go save your ass all over again."

"I had the situation under control," he said coolly.

"No, you didn't. You could at least be honest enough to admit that."

His eyes narrowed as he continued to stare at me. "You're incorrigible."

"Why, thank you. It's one of my better qualities," I said brightly. "And you're changing the subject."

He stiffened, and indignation rippled across his face. "I most certainly am not."

"Are too."

"I refuse to engage in this juvenile dispute."

"Too late. You already did," I told him.

"Let us return to the matter at hand," he said, folding his hands calmly together. "Even if Nyx's lover is the god behind Harker's actions, it is questionable as to whether he would tell her anything about it. The gods don't share everything, even with their lovers."

"They're a lot like angels then." I blushed, realizing what he might imply from that. "I mean about not being big sharers of information. In general. Not specifically about lovers."

Nero laughed—like really laughed. I'd dug such a big hole for myself that I couldn't even see the top anymore, but at least he was enjoying my senseless fumbling. I glared at him.

"Unless you have the magic to back up that glare, I suggest you quit while you're ahead, Pandora," he said with perfect calmness.

"Ahead? You call this ahead?"

He shrugged. "Things can always get worse."

"And on that happy note, I think I'll head to bed now," I said, walking toward the door.

"On your way down, don't forget to pick up the first two books on your list. There will be a quiz tomorrow evening."

I froze in the doorway, then pivoted around. "Are you serious?"

"No, I'm joking. Please pick up a trashy tabloid magazine instead so you can tell me all about Angel Fancy Pants's latest lover. I'm *dying* to know."

He said it with such a straight face that I couldn't help but burst into laughter. I was still chuckling to myself as I checked out *Magic Botany* and *The History and Politics of Witchcraft in New York City* from the library, which drew a disapproving look from the night librarian, a man who defied the librarian stereotype. Well, he was wearing a vest. He just wasn't wearing any shirt under it. As to why he was grumpy, I had no idea. Maybe he didn't approve of fully-clothed people reading books.

I returned to my apartment with my new books in my hands—and, seared into my brain, was the image of the librarian's pierced nipples puckering up under the vest. That piercing must have hurt like hell.

"I thought you were going to see Colonel Sexy Pants," Ivy said as I shut the apartment door behind me.

"I did."

"So you mouthed off to him, and he punished you with homework?"

"No, this isn't punishment homework. It's just regular homework. Tomorrow morning, I'm on Nero's team to visit the New York University of Witchcraft. While he, Captain Somerset, and Jace are grilling the witches about inter-coven disputes, I'm supposed to sneak around to look for evidence that they're behind the poisoning at the Brick Palace."

"Ah, so that's why you and Mr. Brat drank from the Nectar tonight."

"Right."

"Do you want to talk about what happened after that?"

"Which part?"

"The part where Nero Windstriker handcuffed you to his desk."

"No, I don't want to talk about it," I told her.

"Leda, your underwear were on the floor when Drake and I came in."

"Ok, I experienced a moment of Nectar-induced insanity and might have tried to jump Nero's bones."

Ivy laughed. "You two have an interesting relationship."

"We don't have a relationship."

"Uh-huh. Right." She winked at me.

"It was the Nectar," I insisted.

"Honey, the Nectar just made you drunk. It got rid of

your inhibitions. And as soon as those were gone, you made a move on him. What does that tell you?"

I sighed. "Nothing good."

"It's telling you that you're into him."

Yeah, like I needed the Nectar to know that. I knew I was into Nero. But that was a bad thing. A bad, bad thing.

"I have to get some sleep. Tomorrow is going to be a long day," I told Ivy, yawning as I walked toward my room.

I was taking the coward's way out, and I knew it. Then again, being bold had only ever gotten me into trouble. And right now, I had all the trouble I could handle.

CHAPTER 10

WITCH HUNT

*T*he next morning, I changed straight into my leather uniform and headed downstairs to the canteen. I piled eggs, toast, donuts, and cinnamon french toast onto my tray. I just knew it was going to be a long day. Unfortunately, it was not a long breakfast. I had five minutes to eat, and then I had to head down to the underground garage. Nero, Captain Somerset, and Jace were already waiting outside of our car when I got there.

"Get lost, Pandora?" Captain Somerset asked with a smirk.

Nero was far less amused. "You're late," he said.

Actually, according to the clock in the garage, I was exactly ten seconds early, but there was no point in arguing with him. Angel time seemed to operate outside of normal time. Nero opened the door and slid into the driver's seat. Captain Somerset claimed shotgun, leaving the backseat for me and Jace.

The drive passed in silence. Jace kept his face turned away from me the whole time. Either I was sporting some seriously bad body odor, or he was brooding over something. Whatever his reasons for ignoring me, it was better than his previous pattern of trying to beat the crap out of me. Not that he would have dared to do that in Nero's presence without the angel's permission.

Thanks to a lucky break with the stoplights—or Nero manipulating the stoplights—we arrived at the New York University of Witchcraft within minutes. The campus consisted of five large mansions that surrounded a blooming garden where the witches grew all of their potion ingredients. We parked outside Building 1, then we all got out.

There were half a dozen witches in sight, but no one tried to tell us we couldn't park on the sidewalk. They just stood there, their eyes wide with a mix of wonder and shock as Nero led our badass walk toward the entrance. Our steps were perfectly in sync, and our long leather coats swayed majestically in the wind—all that was missing was the heavy beat of an epic soundtrack and the exploding light effects.

Beyond the glass doors that parted in front of us, a grand entrance hall waited. Small glass windows covered the arched ceiling, extending in a nautical swirl halfway down the back wall. A clock sat at the center of that swirl, its gears exposed. Bronze hands announced that it was half past six. Despite the early hour, the hall was not empty. Like the Legion, the witches seemed to be early risers. A woman sat behind a long, curved reception desk that resembled a counter in an apothecary shop. A very chic apothecary shop. The glossy desk was made of cherry wood. At one corner sat an antique bell, and at the other a lovely vase with an orchid plant inside. Orchids, what a perfectly fitting flower for the proper, dignified witches.

The witch behind the desk was certainly just as proper and dignified as the flowers. She wore a dark velvet overcoat with golden fasteners down the front and a matching golden clip in her chin-length black hair. She was busy chatting with the man on the other side of the desk, so neither one had noticed us yet. The male witch wore a brown vest over a blue dress shirt, the sleeves rolled up to the elbows, and a pair of jeans over big cowboy boots. A big brown leather utility belt hung at his hips. A dozen different tools were attached to it. From his outfit, tools, and the bizarre-looking goggles balanced atop his head, he looked like a mechanic. He talked like one too.

"The repairs on the *Flying Siren* are coming along slowly. The airship won't be back up in the air for at least another week," he said.

"Aurora wanted to throw a party aboard the ship on Friday. She won't be happy that it's not ready," the receptionist witch warned him.

"She has her own sister to blame. Her last party…" He shook his head. "I still don't know what they were brewing up there that resulted in them blowing out two of the gas tanks."

"Well, you know how they get when—" The receptionist had just noticed us, hence the dropped jaw.

"Summon the department heads," Nero commanded her.

His wings unfolded behind him as he walked, and the witch's wide eyes panned across the gorgeous tapestry of black, blue, and green feathers. The man was an insufferable showoff, whether or not he cared to admit it, but no one could deny he was strikingly beautiful.

"Now," Nero said, that single crisp word like a punch of magic through the artificially-cooled air.

That broke the witch out of her trance. She grabbed the telephone and hastily began tapping the buttons. The mechanic watched us with a worried expression on his face. We hadn't told the witches we were coming. Nero hadn't wanted to give them any time to prepare for this arbitration —or for the real reason we were here.

While we waited for the illustrious heads of the New York University of Witchcraft to make an appearance, I looked around the reception hall. The red and black checker-board-pattern floor and brick interior walls were a nice touch, but my personal favorite was the Halloween decoration display. The holiday was nearly a month away, but it was not uncommon for witches to spend the entire month of October celebrating.

A mechanical witch made of turning gears stood inside a black cauldron oozing green smoke that smelled like pepper-mint. Pumpkins of all shapes and sizes were piled around the cauldron, and paper jack-o-lanterns hung from the two pillars on either side of the Halloween display. A panel of orange lights blinked 'BOO' over and over again in time to the classical music soundtrack playing in the hall. But it was the row of big, red apples that caught my eye. Someone had taken a bite out of each one, and from those mouth-shaped holes oozed a thick black liquid that was obviously supposed to represent poison. How ironic that poison was precisely what had brought us here.

A door opened, and four witches—three women and one man—stepped into the entrance hall. These four individuals were the most powerful witches in the entire city. Each one of them led one of New York's covens, just as each one of them headed a different department at this university. I'd read all about it in *The History and Politics of Witchcraft in New York City*, one of the books on Nero's reading list. I'd skimmed through most of the slim book last night before bed. I hadn't expected to remember anything when morning came around, but it turned out my retention was better than I'd thought. Maybe I had the gods' second gift to thank for that. Nero had said Witch's Cauldron was a mental gift, not a physical one.

"Colonel Windstriker, what an unexpected pleasure—"

Nero waved his hand, cutting off the witch who'd spoken. I recognized her from the pre-mission reading Nero had assigned me along with the books. Her name was Gwyneth Dorn, and she headed the Steam department at the school. Steam Witches were the inventors and engineers of the witching world. They crafted magic into technology, and it was this Magitech that made the world run smoothly. It powered the cities, the trains, and most importantly, the defenses on the walls that separated humanity from the plains of monsters.

Though Gwyneth's file declared her to be over sixty, she didn't look a day over thirty. Witches weren't immortal, but they did live longer than regular humans. How much longer depended entirely upon how strong their magic was. A powerhouse like Gwyneth could easily live up to two hundred years, meaning she was still in the prime of her life. She was certainly flaunting that for everything it was worth. She wore a dark red corset top with a black ballerina skirt. Her black gloves and the small hat positioned at an artfully slanted angle on the side of her head added a ladylike charm to her outfit, and the piece of black mesh net that covered half of her face gave her a mysterious air.

The man standing to Gwyneth's left was Constantine Wildman, the head of Zoology, the department that studied magical animals and their uses in witchcraft. He was the same age as Gwyneth, but he too showed little evidence of aging. His messy brown hair was almost juvenile, and his outfit of a fitted sweater vest and trekking pants was half professor, half jungle explorer. A gold watch, much like the kind train conductors carried, dangled from his pocket.

Aurora Bennet, the third witch in the group, was in charge of Botany. Her department focused on the study and cultivation of magical plants. She was younger than Gwyneth and Constantine by over thirty years. So was her sister Morgana, who headed the Chemistry department, which specialized in potion-brewing. They were the two sisters who were on the verge of open war.

They looked like twins, though three years separated them. Aurora, the elder of the two, wore a white, lace-trimmed bodice that showed off her cleavage. Her midsection was wrapped inside of a yellow and red corset with dragon patterns sewn into it. The corset ended abruptly at a brown ruffled skirt that was short in the front and long in back. High boots, a leather belt with attached pouches at her hips, and tons of slender silver bracelets topped off her look.

Morgana was dressed more conservatively. She wore striped brown and black tights, black boots, and a body-hugging black top under a brown corset. Her silver hair was dyed with magic, but the spell was slowly wearing off. The tips were already brown. My active mind wondered if she was too busy poisoning people to make time for hair mainte-nance. Only time—and lots of snooping—would tell.

"Aurora Bennet, Morgana Bennet," Nero said after an extended silence.

He'd once told me silence made people uncomfortable, that humans had this innate urge to fill the emptiness—and a sure way to disrupt someone's equilibrium was to not allow them to speak. This worked especially well on people who were used to commanding everyone's attention, like the four witches who headed New York's covens. The look Nero was giving them right now was a dare to speak, and at the same time a promise of what would happen to them if they did.

"This conflict between your covens has escalated beyond

acceptable limits," he told them. "The Legion has decided to step in. We will determine who is guilty and who will be punished." The hard look in his eyes expanded to include Gwyneth and Constantine too. "You have ten minutes to summon the students and staff to the assembly hall for questioning."

"*All* of them?" Aurora said, her jaw clenched.

"Every last witch."

"But that will disrupt our students' course schedules," Gwyneth protested with indignation.

"You seem to be under the misconception that I am asking," Nero replied coldly. "I'm telling you. And you will obey. Go."

The force in his voice snapped like a bolt of lightning, sending the witches scrambling. As soon as the four department heads were gone, he turned to the gaping mechanic. From the look on the man's face, he'd never seen those witches jump for anyone.

"Show us to the assembly hall," Nero commanded him. "And I'm going to need you to procure a few things for me before we begin the hearing."

————

I SNUCK OUT OF THE ASSEMBLY HALL BEFORE THE WITCH hearing began. While the university's professors and students were being grilled on anything and everything that had to do with the hostilities between the covens of Aurora and Morgana, I walked the empty grounds in search of a darker threat. The Chemistry labs in Building 2 were my first stop. If the witches were brewing up trouble, that's where I'd find the evidence.

Unsurprisingly, there was no book marked 'Evidence' set

out in clear sight for me to find, but there were inventory and restocking reports tucked away in the office that stood at the nexus of the labs. I scanned the pages for any mention of Sunset Pollen or Snapdragon Venom, the two substances we'd found in the residue at the Brick Palace. To avoid being seen, I kept the room's lights off, but that also made it harder to read. It was a good thing I had supernatu-rally-enhanced vision—and that I'd deactivated the surveillance in the area. The latest Magitech cameras, which I had to assume the witches had, didn't need much light to see.

I'd made it through most of the reports in the cabinet when blinding white light flooded the office. The sharp clicks of high heels against the tiled floor sent me scrambling for cover inside the nearest lab. Officially, the witches couldn't do anything to me if they found me here, but that wouldn't stop them from unofficially blowing me up and burning my remains. Plus, if they figured out what we were doing before I had a chance to collect evidence, we might never learn who was behind the poisoning.

The footsteps were still headed my way. I drew my gun and waited behind the door. My weapon was loaded with magic-made tranquilizers. Nero had told me to neutralize anyone who discovered me. I chose to believe he meant stun them. I was not going to kill a person simply because they'd had the misfortune to walk in on me while I was snooping. The lab lights flashed to life now, and I aimed the gun at the door…

I froze when I saw the person who'd just stepped into the lab. "Bella," I said, coming out of hiding.

My sister turned toward me, her eyes flickering from my face to the gun still in my hands. "Leda, I hope you're not here to shoot me."

"That depends. Are you an evil witch planning to kill everyone in the city?"

The horrified expression on her face was answer enough, not that I'd ever doubted her. Bella was too gentle to hurt anyone. She simply didn't have the temperament for world domination. She was a sweet person but a horrible liar. Back at home, I'd always known when she was hiding something. Every twitch, every glance, every step had been a dead give-away, and that had been *before* I'd drunk the Nectar of the gods and added supernatural senses to my arsenal of lie-detection skills.

I holstered my gun and shot her a grin. "How could I shoot my favorite sister?"

A smile slowly spread across her lips. "Don't tell Gin or Tessa."

I laughed. "They're seventeen, not stupid. I'm sure they know you're my favorite. And besides, they're each other's favorite sister. You can't break a bond formed from a mutual love of shopping."

"I've missed your irreverent commentary, Leda." Bella rushed forward, embracing me. She hugged me so hard that she pushed the air right out of me. "It's been too long." She gave me a final squeeze before letting go.

"Just two months," I told her, stepping back to get a better look at her. She was wearing a pale blue blouse that brought out her eyes, and a hip-hugging knee-length skirt that brought out her curves. "You are a powerful witch now."

"I'm still working on it," she replied, blushing.

"I've read your letters, Bella. You might be too modest to boast, but I could read between the lines well enough. You're at the top of your class."

"This is a marvelous place," she said, her eyes going dreamy. "I'm learning so much."

I couldn't help but smile. "I'm glad. You've wanted to study here since we were kids, and now you're finally here."

"Because of you. I was only able to study here because of you. For two years, you worked extra jobs to pay for my first semester's tuition, and now…" A tear rolled down her cheek. "Leda, Calli told me what you did."

"Whatever it was, it wasn't me."

"A few days ago, you paid my tuition bill for the entire two years."

I shrugged. "I got my first paycheck and had nothing to spend it on. The Legion already provides my food and board. And I figured you needed the money more than I needed a dragon-skin purse."

More tears poured from her eyes. "I love you, Leda."

"And I love you. I've missed you so much."

"I take it that is not the reason for your visit?"

"No."

"You're here with the Legion contingent led by Colonel Windstriker."

"Yes."

A smirk touched her red lips. "Aha."

"Aha what?"

"Calli told me about the Colonel. I see that she's right."

"Right about what?"

Her smile grew wider. "That you're into him." I rolled my eyes, but that only made her laugh. "I saw him. He's cute."

"You wouldn't be saying that if you'd had to survive his training sessions for the past two months."

"You survived it, and you *are* saying it," she countered.

"I haven't said any such thing."

"Not with your lips perhaps, but your eyes tell all." She reached out to squeeze my hand. "So, why are you here when the rest of the Legion contingent and everyone else is in the assembly hall?"

"Not everyone," I said. "You're here."

"We were just dismissed for lunch."

Was it already so late? One glance up at the clock was all it took to realize that I'd completely lost track of time. I had read through three-quarters of the inventory reports and seen no mention of either Sunset Pollen or Snapdragon Venom. It was possible that I'd find a report about them in the remaining folders, but I seriously doubted it.

"Your angel has adjourned the meeting for one hour," Bella continued.

"He's not *my* angel."

Her brows lifted, but she didn't tease me further. "This morning, university security barged into the lab to herd us all into the assembly hall. I came back to grab the book I forgot here." She took the textbook lying on the tabletop.

"Are these the only labs in the university?" I asked Bella.

"These are the labs the students use." Her mouth hardened with suspicion. "You're not really here about Aurora and Morgana, are you?"

"That remains to be seen," I said. "Have they been acting strangely?"

"You mean like crashing each other's parties? Or sabotaging each other's workspaces? They are two grown women fighting over resources, rituals, and perceived slights, Leda. Worse yet, they are sisters. They should be looking out for each other, not spending their days inventing new and horrible ways to stab each other in the back. And everyone is suffering because of it. I'd be glad the Legion had stepped in, if I weren't sure you're here for some other reason." She gave me a loaded look.

"You're right," I said, keeping my voice low. "Did you

hear about what happened at the Brick Palace a couple days ago?"

"Yeah, the building caught on fire. Nearly a hundred people died. How horrible."

"They died before the fire. Someone rigged the cooling system to expel poison. We found traces of Sunset Pollen and Snapdragon Venom in the residue inside the building."

"Those substances are only made at this university. That's why you're here. You think someone here poisoned those people." Her gloved hand flitted to her mouth.

"As you said, both substances are only made here," I said. "Do you know where they're kept?"

"Morgana and the Chemistry professors have their own lab on the second floor. We're not allowed in there, but everyone knows it's where they keep the really interesting things, Sunset Pollen and Snapdragon Venom among them."

It looked like I'd be sneaking into the second floor Chemistry lab after lunch.

"No, the entire second floor is protected by wards," Bella said, guessing my thoughts. "It's where all the restricted-access rooms are."

So much for sneaking. I didn't think I could bypass a ward made by a witch coven leader. Their magic was too strong.

"Leda," Bella said quietly. "Why would witches kill all of those people?"

"I don't know," I replied. "But we think whoever killed them might be working for demons."

"Demons." She hissed the word like it was a curse.

"Demons can grant supernaturals new and powerful magic. If a witch wanted a way to gain a power advantage over another witch, that is one way to do it."

"By dealing with a demon?" Bella shook her head. "No, I can't believe anyone here would do that."

"You always see the good in people," I said, smiling at her. "But everyone has their own inner demons, Bella. Some people just wear them closer to the surface."

"That's a very cynical attitude to have."

"I need to play the cynic right now if I'm going to catch this murderer. You can help me."

"How?" she asked.

"You can help me think this through. You've always been good at that."

"Whatever you need."

"So, if Morgana was the one who made the poison, if she did it to gain an edge over her sister, why would she use Sunset Pollen and Snapdragon Venom? What is special about those substances?" I asked her.

"Despite their misleading names, both poisons are made from animals, not plants. Morgana's sister Aurora is the head of the Botany department. Morgana wouldn't go to her sister's people for poisons. They'd tell Aurora, Aurora would figure out why, and then the game would be up. Assuming Morgana is the one behind this," she added hastily.

"Constantine Wildman is the head of Zoology," I said. "What if he's in on this too?"

"Then the university is in big trouble. If Morgana and Constantine are in on this together, the demons could easily infiltrate the entire school."

"Have you seen any evidence of that?"

"No, but they wouldn't openly flaunt it, would they? We have to figure out which witch is behind this."

"Or which witches," I added. "Does that mean you'll help me?"

"Leda, you know you don't even have to ask. I will always help you, whatever you need."

The clocktower outside began to ring out a melody of bells and beats.

"The meal bells," she said. "Lunch is starting in the restaurant."

I linked my arm in hers. "How about you show me to the restaurant?"

I'd memorized the university blueprints Nero had given me, but I wasn't going to miss a chance for some sisterly bonding. It had been far too long. We walked arm-in-arm to the restaurant in Building 1, chatting the whole way. Happiness tumbled with sorrow inside of me. My heart ached for those happy, golden days—the days when we'd all been together. We might catch a fleeting moment here and there, but those days would never truly come again.

"So, tell me about the guy you're seeing," I said, smiling past the painful twinges inside my chest.

"How did you know?" she asked, shocked.

"There's a certain glow around you. Dare I guess it's love?"

"I'm not sure what it is." Happiness washed across her face. "But it feels good."

"Good." I tightened my hold on her arm. "Because if anyone deserves to be happy, it's you."

"Leda, you deserve happiness most of all." Her voice dropped to a whisper as we stepped into a hallway full of witches. "Your selfless sacrifice…"

We'd entered the restaurant, so we spoke no more of sacrifices or other serious matters. Bella gave my hand a squeeze before joining a group of witches at one of the tables.

The restaurant possessed the same elegant blend of modern and nostalgic elements—and of magic and technology—that characterized the witches. Gold curtains and antique wood furniture. Top-of-the-line coffee machines and blenders. Silver and porcelain, silk and stainless steel. It was so beautiful that I could have stared all day, but there was no time for that. I had to find Nero and the others.

I'd no sooner had the thought than they stepped into the restaurant. Nero led them across the room like he owned everything in it. Every plate and fork, every table and flower vase. And every person. The witches turned to stare at him in wonder. There was something darkly sensual about the way he possessed any space he entered, and I couldn't help but stare a little myself. How did he do it? No one had looked at me like that when I'd come in with Bella.

"If you want to own any room you're in, then you have to *believe* you own it," he said as I moved into step beside them.

The more time we spent together, the easier it was getting for him to read my thoughts. I needed to learn to block him better. Or, better yet, I should stop spending so much time with him. That's what any sane and logical person would do.

"What were you discussing with your sister?" he asked.

"We were just catching up."

We moved into a private dining room at the far end of the restaurant. Soft orchestra music played from the speakers on the walls. We took our chairs around the dining room table, which was large enough to seat four times our numbers. Waiters in tuxedos rushed to fill our water glasses. When they were finished, Nero waved them away. Smooth as silk, they fluttered from the room and shut the door behind them.

Nero took a roll from the bread basket, his eyes staring at me from across the table. "I hope your familial entanglements won't keep you from doing your job."

"Of course not."

"Your sister is a witch."

"Really? I hadn't noticed, but thank you for bringing it to my attention."

Jace nearly choked on his roll, while Captain Somerset looked from me to Nero with obvious amusement.

"Careful," Nero warned me.

I took a bite out of my roll before my mouth got me into trouble.

"Wise choice," he said.

The doors opened again, and the four waiters glided in like they were skating across ice. They set a tiny plate of very snooty-looking pasta in front of each of us, then left the room again. I poked at the pretentious arrangement of carrots beside the two ravioli pouches on my plate.

"Afraid your lunch will try to eat you, Pandora?" Captain Somerset teased.

"No. It's just…something feels weird." There was an odd charge to the air, like static popping against my skin. A low hum buzzed in my ears.

"Shall we call the kitchen to order you something more to your liking?" She smirked. "Perhaps a bowl of macaroni and cheese?"

"That's not what I meant. It's just…" I shook my head. "I don't know what it is."

And before I could figure it out, an explosion shook the room.

CHAPTER 11

THE BRINGER OF CHAOS

*J*ace slammed into me, throwing me to the floor as furniture exploded all around us. Smoke saturated the air, stinging my eyes and burning my throat. I blinked and looked up into Jace's face.

"Uh, thanks," I said. Why had he thrown himself over me? He hated me.

We stood and looked around. There wasn't much left of the room. The furniture was in pieces, the window shattered, and the carpet burning. Nero waved his hand, and a fresh breeze blew in through the demolished window, putting out the fire and dispersing the smoke. Captain Somerset was already picking through the debris.

Nero had his phone out. "There's been an incident," he said brusquely. "Send me the bomb squad and an inquisition team." Then he hung up. "Let's go," he told me and Jace.

"What do you want us to do?" I asked him.

"We're going to keep an eye on those witches until the inquisition team arrives to interrogate them."

"What if the people who set the bomb are already gone?"

"That is unlikely. I put a magic barrier around the

campus," he said. "No one is getting in or out unless I allow it."

"You put a barrier around the whole campus?" I gasped.

"Yes," he said, as though it were no big deal.

"How long can you hold the barrier?"

"Long enough."

We headed toward the door. The bomb had gone off on the other side of the room, which was probably the only reason the door was still standing. I took a glance at the bomb debris. The boom had certainly been impressively loud, and the furniture had exploded spectacularly, but it all seemed so…cosmetic.

"That bomb wasn't supposed to kill us, was it?" I asked him.

"No."

"It was a warning," I realized. "Someone knows what we're doing here, and they're warning us to stay away. Who is even crazy enough to threaten the Legion of Angels?"

"I don't know," he said. "But whoever it is, they will soon wish they'd killed us instead."

———

Rather than spending my afternoon trying to sneak into those restricted access labs on the second floor as planned, I found myself heading back to the Legion. Nero and Captain Somerset were still back at the university supervising the hundred or so soldiers who'd arrived to investigate the bombing in the dining room. Even though Jace and I weren't staying behind, that didn't mean we were off the hook. Nero had instructed us to spend the afternoon training in Hall Six.

Hall Six was one of the Legion's smaller gym halls. It

didn't have space for complex obstacle courses or large group exercises. It was better suited for one-on-one training. So that's what we did. For hours, Jace and I dueled with swords and knives and sticks, each weapon in turn. And then we dueled hand-to-hand, or fist-to-face on my end. Though I'd improved a lot since joining the Legion, Jace was still a lot better than I was. I was a big enough person to admit that— but just not out loud.

"You're getting better," Jace commented when we took a break to sit on the floor and gulp down water.

"Are you just trying to make me feel better?" I asked, rubbing my sore ribs.

"That's not my style."

"Of course not." I snorted. "I forgot. You hate me."

"I don't hate you, Leda."

Leda was it? He'd never called me by my actual name before. He and the other Legion brats had adopted Nero's nickname for me: Pandora, the bringer of chaos. So what had changed? What was going on with Jace?

"You don't hate me," I repeated with disbelief. "Right."

"You saved my life," he said. "I've been nothing but awful to you, but back in the Brick Palace when it was on fire, you saved me. You could have left me there to die, but you didn't. Why?"

"Because you don't just leave people to die, no matter how much of an asshole they've been to you."

He watched me for a few moments, as though he didn't know what to make of me. "You aren't like other people."

I laughed, and he frowned at me.

"I'm serious," he said. "It's not normal to care about people who've been mean to you."

"Ok, so now I'm not normal?"

"That's not what I meant. I just meant…" His usual hard

arrogance cracked, leaking the uncertainty that lay within. "We're competitors."

"How do you figure that?"

"There are only so many spots at the top of the Legion. Some fail, some succeed. The more other people who succeed, the more competition you have for those spots. We can't all be angels."

"What makes you think I want to be an angel?"

"You wouldn't push yourself so hard if you didn't want to make it to the top," he said. "You train harder than anyone, even me. And it shows. You've already passed most of my fellow brats."

I looked at him in surprise.

A slight smile touched his lips. "Yeah, I know the term. Oh, did you think your friend Ivy came up with it herself? The children of angels have been called 'Legion brats' since there have been children of angels. And we don't mind the term. On the contrary, we wear it as a badge of honor. Each and every one of us is proud of our family's legacy."

"Maybe pride is the problem," I said. "You consider anyone outside your prestigious circle a potential threat. The paranoia must be exhausting."

"Yes," he agreed. "You're right. We would be much happier if we weren't so competitive." He sighed. "But then we wouldn't be who we are, would we?"

"You're pretty philosophical for a brat," I told him, smirking.

He returned the smirk. "And you're surprisingly alive for someone who mouths off to an angel. Regularly."

"It must be my infinite charm and wit that's saved me from his wrath."

Jace snorted. "One of these days, your luck is going to run out. You're not afraid of anything, are you?"

"Oh, no. I'm not going to spill my secrets and give your competitive side the chance to use them against me."

"Well, it was worth a try," he said with an easy shrug. "You did a really brave thing back on the Black Plains, by the way. Brave but crazy."

"That is Pandora's favorite combination."

We both turned toward the door. Nero stood there, his arms folded over his chest, his eyes hard.

"Colonel Windstriker," Jace said, scrambling to his feet.

Nero looked past him, his eyes panning with me as I rose slowly from the floor. Mischief flared up in me, and I shot him a wicked smile.

"I ordered you to train," he said coolly.

Jace didn't respond, so I spoke for the both of us. "We've spent the last four hours training. I can show you my bruised ribs to prove it." My hand lifted to my sore right side.

"There is no need to remove your clothing at this time."

A low grunt shook Jace's chest.

Nero turned his hard stare on him. "Is something funny, Corporal Fireswift?"

Jace put the stopper on the chuckles, molding his face into an expressionless block. "No, sir."

"Good," Nero said, his eyes shifting to me. "Show me what you've been practicing."

I turned toward Jace. Slowly, we began to circle each other.

"I hope you haven't spent the last four hours playing Ring-Around-the-Rosie," Nero said sharply.

At his words, Jace surged forward. I knew he would target my injured ribs. With Nero watching, he wanted to make this quick and clean. Our surprisingly civil chat didn't change the fact that he saw me as a threat to be taken down.

Well, I wasn't going to make it that easy for him. I waited

until he was nearly upon me, then I pivoted, kicking the back of his legs as he passed me. Jace stumbled, but he recovered immediately. He spun around so fast that I couldn't react in time. His fist hammered into me, and I doubled over from the fresh stab of pain to my ribs. I straightened, but I was too slow. Jace's second blow hit me hard in the face. I snapped my head up, blood pouring out of my nose. I caught his fist on its next swing and twisted it behind his back. My hold on him was too slippery, however, and he flipped me over him, throwing me.

"Move faster, Pandora," Nero called as my back smacked against the floor.

I didn't have any spare energy to curse at him, so I focused on getting back up again. My bones groaned in agony when I jumped to my feet. The whole world seemed to tip like a ship caught in a storm. I blinked back the blackness creeping across my vision and turned to face Jace. His next sequence of punches streaked across my already-blurred vision, but I managed to avoid his fists at least.

"Stop running away and fight," Nero chided me from the sidelines.

"Stop distracting me," I ground out.

Jace's leg swung low, tripping me. I rolled to avoid his followup stomp and my leg bumped against a water bottle. Grabbing the full bottle, I jumped up and launched it at Jace's head. It hit him square between the eyes. I took advantage of his brief moment of shock to rush him, tackling him to the ground. As we touched down, I flipped him over to plant him face-first against the floor. I pulled back on his arms, and he grunted in pain. He tried to thrash free, but I'd pinned him too well.

"Stop," Nero said, and Jace stopped struggling. "Let him up," he told me.

I released Jace, and we both got to our feet.

"Your performance was satisfactory. You may go," Nero said to Jace.

Nero waited until he was gone, then he turned his eyes on me. He maintained a cold, silent stare until I couldn't stand it any longer.

"Ok, what is it?" I said. "What did I do wrong?"

His eyes hardened. "You tell me."

"He's too strong, so I can't let him get in so many blows," I said, wiping the blood from my face.

Nero's eyes flickered briefly to the blood on my hands. "Yes, you need to move faster or get more resilient. Preferably both. What else?"

"I got slippery hands?"

He sighed.

And so did I. "Gods, Nero, why don't you just spit it out?"

"This."

Something shot at my head. I threw up my hands and caught the water bottle I'd used in my last fight. Nero had moved so fast that I hadn't even seen him pick it up.

"This is a water bottle," he stated.

"Why thank you for telling me, Mr. Obvious. Or should I call you Colonel Obvious?" I winked at him.

"A water bottle is not a weapon," he continued.

"It is the way I used it."

"You know how I feel about your improvised weapons."

"That they are clever?"

"This isn't funny," he told me.

"It is from where I'm standing," I replied with a smirk.

"Let's see if I can't change that." He motioned me forward.

"I don't let men spank me until the second date."

"What has made you so bold?"

I was asking myself the same thing. Part of it was my mouth's tendency to fire off whenever Nero was around, but that wasn't all. I'd nearly been blown to pieces today. Ok, if we were right, the bomb had never meant to kill us, just scare us, but that didn't mean we couldn't have died. There was something about facing my own mortality and surviving that made me feel oddly immortal—and bold.

"What has made you so hard on me?" I shot back, embracing the boldness.

"I'm always hard on people."

"You weren't hard on Jace."

"He didn't fight his opponent with a water bottle."

"Maybe that's why he lost."

Nero caught my wrist. "No, he lost because you've done something to him." He wiped the blood from my hand with a towel, then released me.

"What did I do to him?" I asked.

He tossed the towel aside. "You were kind to him."

"And that's a bad thing?"

"You reminded him of something we Legion brats have been trained from birth to forget," he said.

"Which is?"

"That we're human. When you treated him with kindness, Leda, you made him care about you. You made him more human."

"Are we talking about Jace or you?" I asked him.

He ignored my question. "And at that moment, he ceased to be the merciless soldier he is supposed to be. Between the two of you, he is the superior fighter. He could have beaten you many times over during the course of your duel, and yet you won. Because he didn't press his advantage. You have made him weaker."

"So basically you're accusing me of ruining a perfectly good soldier."

"No, I'm blaming him for letting you," he told me, his eyes burning with emotion.

I still couldn't help but think that we were really talking about Nero, but I said nothing. If he was afraid I made him too human, then any relationship between us was doomed from the beginning. That bothered me more than it should have. Didn't I want to avoid a relationship that would only end in heartache? The problem was that a small part of me refused to believe our relationship was doomed—and despite my best efforts, that small part was growing.

"Now," Nero said, all traces of emotion gone from his eyes. "Let's see how well you hold up against someone who isn't distracted by flying water bottles."

CHAPTER 12

*N*ero spent the next hour showing me what it meant to have no mercy or humanity. His argument was a convincing one. I certainly believed in his merciless inhumanity while he was adding fresh injuries to the ones Jace had inflicted on me, but then he healed me at the end. The cynic in me told me that he just wanted me to live to fight another day. That small, hopeful voice disagreed; it decided he wanted to spare me the pain of bruised bones. This time, my cynical side won the argument. He'd kicked my ass so thoroughly that the memories of the pain lingered on long after his magic had healed my body.

When I got back to my apartment, Ivy was bustling around the living room, clearly agitated. Her mood was in stark opposition to her very put-together outfit: a green short-sleeved sweater dress paired with brown leather boots and a matching belt.

"What's wrong?" I asked her.

She spun around to face me as I closed the door behind me. "Have you seen my brown purse? I can't find it anywhere, and I'm late."

"Did you look in the refrigerator?"

"The refrigerator?" she asked, her red eyebrows drawing together as she power-walked to Drake's mini fridge. "Why would it be…" Her confusion only deepened when she found her purse inside. "This is weird. How did it get in there? And how did you know it was in there?"

"Drake was experimenting this morning," I told her. "I guess he forgot to take it out."

Ivy shook her head. "Do I want to know what this experiment was and why he needed my purse for it?"

"I don't even know what he was doing."

Ivy peeked inside her purse. "Well, it looks the same as before." With that said, her usual smile returned. "Ok, I am —" She froze, her eyes panning up and down me. "What happened to you?"

"We almost got blown up by witches, then I trained with Jace for four hours until Nero came back to further kick my ass."

"You're bleeding!"

"Not anymore. It's old blood. It's all dry by now."

Rather than appeasing her, my words only seemed to make things worse. "Your day sucked."

"Yeah," I agreed. "It really did."

"Well, don't just stand there. We're going to turn it right around. Get cleaned up and changed, and then you're coming with me to Three Wishes."

"Three Wishes?"

"It's a club," she said. "There's a party going on tonight, and I'm bringing you."

"I thought you were late."

"Fashionably late, and we both are," she said, nudging me toward my room. "Come on."

"Is this a Legion club?" I asked her as I began to put on the clothes she was pulling out of my closet.

"No, it's a fairy club."

"Good."

"Good?" she asked.

"Yes."

"Ah." Her eyes lit up in understanding. "You're not avoiding a certain angel, are you?"

Yes. "I just thought it would be nice to get away from the rigidity of the Legion for a bit."

"Uh-huh." I could tell she wasn't fooled. "Well, it's just a small group of us going to Three Wishes. There shouldn't be anyone else from the Legion. A few of the Legion clubs are having a party tonight, so everyone will be at those, not where we're going."

Thank goodness. I finished dressing in record time, then said, "Ok. Show me to this angel-free party zone."

———

THREE WISHES WASN'T AS EXTRAVAGANT AS THE LEGION clubs. It didn't have marble floors, diamond sculptures, or fancy light shows. The club was rather rustic actually. The wood floor creaked, and the furniture was etched with the chips and scratches of time. And rather than a high-end, Magitech-powered stereo system, a live band played on the raised stage.

In one word, the fairy club was *perfect*.

Ivy had been right. Except for her date, the now-Captain Diaz, and half a dozen others she'd invited, there wasn't a single Legion soldier to be found inside Three Wishes. After a round of sparkling shots, we played our way through the game stations all around the club. There was pool and air hockey and darts. For a dollar, we could even arm-wrestle a werewolf. A muscular man with chin-length hair and a two-day beard, the werewolf grinned at me when I sat down opposite him, but his smile faded the moment he realized I wasn't as weak as he'd thought.

"You're pretty strong for a little girl," he said through clenched teeth as I slowly forced his arm toward the table. He inhaled deeply, drinking in my scent. "You're not a fairy. What are you?"

"You're wrestling a soldier of the Legion," Ivy told him with a bright smile.

"Hmm." He took another whiff.

"Do you mind?" I said. "That's kind of creepy."

"It's how I sense magic, sweetness." His voice was as rough as sandpaper. "What level are you?"

"Two."

He sniffed me again. "You smell like angel."

"That's her boyfriend you're smelling," Ivy said.

"Boyfriend?"

Surprise froze him, and I took advantage. I pushed harder, slamming his arm against the table.

"You distracted him," said Captain Diaz. No, Soren. He'd insisted I call him Soren. I wondered if that would change if he ever ended up in charge of training us.

Ivy shrugged. "And? If he got distracted, that's his problem. Leda won fair and square. Hey, what did she win?" she asked the werewolf.

"What would you like as your prize?" he asked me.

"She'd like to dance with you," Ivy answered for me.

I turned to glower at her, but the werewolf had already wrapped his arm around my back. I allowed him to lead me to the dance floor. Why not? One dance wouldn't kill me. Even if he wanted to bite me—which didn't seem likely from the way he was looking at me—soldiers of the Legion were immune to werewolf venom. And, besides, he was kind of ruggedly handsome. I didn't mind dancing with him.

"What's your name?" he asked me, settling his hands on my hips.

"Leda." I balanced my arms over his shoulders. Where else was I supposed to put them? We were so close that we were practically dancing cheek-to-cheek.

"I'm Stash." His lips spread into a smile. "Pleased to meet you, Leda."

"So," I said. "What is a big bad wolf doing arm-wrestling people inside a fairy club?" His smile vanished, telling me I'd asked the wrong thing. "Sorry, I didn't mean to pry."

"No, it's a valid question. I am a sideshow in this fairy carnival because I need the cash, and most shifters outright refuse to hire me ever since my pack kicked me out."

I didn't ask why they'd kicked him out. That would definitely be prying. So I was surprised when he told me himself.

"The alpha and I had a difference of opinion. And I don't know how to keep my mouth shut. I'm not the good, obedient wolf."

"Neither am I. An obedient soldier, I mean," I added quickly.

"Is that why you're here instead of out with Colonel Windstriker?" he asked me.

I looked at him in surprise.

"There's only one angel living in New York," he said.

"Nero is not my boyfriend," I told him.

His mouth lifted in a smile. "It's only a matter of time, sweetness."

"Why do people keep saying that?" I growled.

"Your eyes light up and your scent changes when you talk about him."

"I…" I didn't know what to say to that. "Let's just not talk about him, ok?"

"As you wish."

A new song started, this one peppier than the last, and then a loud, off-key voice belted out the lyrics to *Supernatural Fever* over the microphone. I turned my head toward the stage, where Lyle, one of our Legion buddies, was singing karaoke to the amusement of our entire group.

"Apparently, singing isn't one of the gods' gifts to the Legion," Stash commented.

I snorted. "Definitely not."

"Thank you for the dance," he said. "And now I must get back to work."

"Try not to lose to anyone else. Or you'll be dancing all night." I glanced at the long line of women waiting in front of his table. They were all staring across the dance floor at him, starry-eyed expressions on their faces as they jiggled one-dollar bills at him. It appeared the werewolf had a fan club.

Stash winked at me, then headed over to greet his adoring fans. I found Ivy upstairs sitting on a sofa that overlooked the club's lower floor. As soon as Lyle had finished singing, he joined us. We were soon all sore with laughter thanks to the cheesy comedy skits the fairies were acting out on the stage. One skit ended, and the lights dimmed. Two men stepped onto the stage—one in torn jeans and a dirty t-shirt, the other in a suit of shiny black leather.

"Who are you?" the ragged man asked the other.

"How can you not know me, mortal?" The man in the leather bodysuit straightened with indignation, and paper wings burst out of his back. "I am the great and powerful Nero Windstriker, angel of New York, the gods' hand of justice." His wings retracted, then burst out again, exploding into confetti.

The other man looked Fake Nero up and down, then declared, "I thought you'd be taller."

"Height matters not. Only the power of the gods. I could kill you where you stand without lifting a finger."

"Except he'd never do that, would he, Leda?" Ivy whispered to me. "He prefers to use his hands." She wiggled her eyebrows up and down.

"I'm going to pretend I didn't hear that," Soren told her. "Or see that." He made a point of looking away from the stage. His expression was masked, but I could tell he was laughing inside. The rest of us didn't bother to contain the chuckles—more at the ludicrousness of the skit than at anything else.

"Tell me of your great deeds, oh powerful one," Mere Mortal said down on the stage. "Is it true you can move objects with your mind?"

"Of course." Fake Nero lifted his hands, and the rocks on the stage rose into the air. I could see the shimmer of the transparent wires, but that didn't detract from the fun.

"And you can control the elements themselves?" asked Mere Mortal.

"Ha! That is child's play," Fake Nero said as fake flames burst to life on the chair beside him and the stage floor began to rumble. "Whether fire or ice, air or earth, I am the master of—" He froze, and so did the cheesy effects.

"Don't stop on my account," a familiar voice said.

I leaned forward over the banister to see the real Nero walking across the club. People parted before him, a mix of wonder and fear shining in their eyes. He took a seat on the sofa in front of the stage. Captain Somerset sat down beside him. What were they doing here?

"Continue," Nero told the actors. "Do tell me more about my great and powerful magic."

The room was so silent I could almost hear the sands of time pouring out. Then the lights over the stage faded out. The two actors shuffled away, and when the lights flared up again, a choir of men and women in long robes were standing in neat rows. They opened their mouths and began to sing. Their song was so eerily beautiful that it took me a few verses to realize it was a hymn from the Book of the Gods—and then I nearly laughed. Their hasty attempt to appease Nero was funnier than all of the comedy skits that had come before it. It was even funnier than Lyle's karaoke. And it proved that they didn't understand Nero at all. He wasn't moved by songs or praise or outward displays of piety. No, if the angel of New York was moved by anything, it was action.

"You sure are a mood killer," I heard Captain Somerset chuckle during a lull in the hymn.

"I told them to continue," replied Nero.

"No one is brave enough to make fun of you to your face. Well, except Pandora."

I leaned back. They hadn't seen me yet, and I wanted to keep it that way.

"What are they doing here?" I hissed at Ivy. "I thought the officers of the Legion had their own fancy parties going on tonight."

Ivy glanced at Soren, who said, "We do. I decided to forgo those festivities in favor of sweeter company." He flashed her a charming smile and wrapped his arm around her.

"Wise man," she said, resting her head on his shoulder.

"It looks like they had the same idea," he told me, his eyes flickering to the lower club.

I followed his gaze to the two fairies who'd just stopped in front of Nero's sofa. One of the fairies was pink—like *really* pink, from head to toe. Pink hair tied up into a high ponytail. A pink sequin dress with a frilly pink chiffon skirt. Pink gemstones dangling from her bracelets. And pink slippers, of course.

Where Miss Pink was pink, her friend was blue. She had chin-length blue hair, a sequin cocktail dress that shimmered like an undersea light show, and blue slippers with blue ribbons that criss-crossed up her legs, ending in big bows at her knees.

Captain Somerset waved the two fairies forward, and they slid onto the sofa, Miss Blue to her and Miss Pink to Nero. A double date. So that's why they'd come here. Now, wasn't that just kill-me-with-a-machete awesome. As Miss Pink climbed onto Nero's lap, my party high crashed.

"I have to go," I told Ivy. "Early morning tomorrow."

I turned away from the pitying look she gave me. There was no reason for her to feel sorry for me. I was an adult. I could handle this. As I walked down the stairs, I concentrated on how early I'd have to wake up tomorrow for training. Suddenly, the prospect of Nero kicking my ass from one end of the gym hall to the other at five in the morning didn't sound all that appealing.

My path to the exit would bring me right past Nero's love seat. Luckily for me, right now he was busy looking at the fairy whose hands were all over him. Gritting my teeth, I skirted the edge of the stairs, hoping to avoid notice. Captain Somerset and Miss Blue were making out like there was no tomorrow, but as Miss Pink dipped her mouth to kiss Nero, his head snapped to me. His stare bore into me, his eyes burning with an emerald fire so intense that I felt the temperature in the room rise. Invisible flames licked my skin, enveloping my whole body, drowning me in a fever that just couldn't break.

His mouth parted, and his tongue flicked out, tracing his lower lip so slowly that time seemed to stop. A warning screamed inside my head, unfreezing me. I turned and ran out of there, not looking back.

Nero's date shouldn't bother me. Really it shouldn't. So why did it? Why did I care? What was wrong with me? I growled in frustration. I really needed to get my mind off that angel. And I had just the trick. I pulled out my phone and called Bella.

"Hey, Leda," she answered on the first ring. "How are you?"

Crushed. Broken. Furious. "I'm fine," I told her. "Do you still want to help me get to the bottom of the poisoning at the Brick Palace?"

"Of course. How can I help?"

"We're going to break into Morgana's lab."

CHAPTER 13

POISON AND STEAM

*A*fter a quick stop at my apartment to change into something more appropriate for breaking and entering—and another stop at Nerissa's lab to beg for something that could assist me with said breaking and entering—I headed back to the New York University of Witchcraft. The school looked creepier at night than it had during the day, either thanks to the spindly silhouette of naked trees against the full moon or just thanks to my nerves.

I can do this, I told myself. *Back in my bounty hunter days, I did things like this all the time.*

Except I'd never broken into a high-security house of witches who might be in league with demons. The Legion hadn't sanctioned this mission either, and Nero would be pissed off if he found out. He'd be less angry if my mission produced results, so that's what I was going to focus on right now. This investigation was going nowhere. It was high time someone changed that.

I met Bella outside of Building 2. It was nearly midnight and everyone was tucked inside the dormitory building for the night—or was out partying at the clubs. No one was working in the labs on a Friday night, Bella assured me, and she was right. As we walked down the dark corridor and up the spiral staircase to the second floor, we didn't see a single soul.

A glowing curtain of magic barred passage to the hallway of labs. I pulled out a spiffy little piece of Magitech I'd gotten from Nerissa. As long as I held it, I and anyone I touched could pass through any ward a witch could make. At least according to Nerissa. Well, we were about to learn if she was right. I held my breath when Bella and I passed through the green curtain, but even though I felt the spell nipping at the shield around us, it didn't touch us.

"Ok," I said, exhaling in relief once we were past the barrier. "Let's check out Morgana's Chemistry lab for the poisons we found at the Brick Palace."

Bella pulled a small box out of her pocket. She waved her hand over it, and the cube's smooth white sides began to glow yellow.

"That's a neat trick," I told her as we entered the lab. A quick look around told me all of the cameras were off. Odd.

"Light in a Box," she said with a smile. "I can teach it to you if you want."

"I'm not a witch."

"But you do have the powers of a witch. You gained the gods' second gift, the gift of witchcraft, didn't you?"

"Yes, but I haven't been able to spell so much as a matchstick yet."

She chuckled softly.

"What is it?" I asked her.

"That little piece of Magitech you used to get us past the barrier can only be activated by a witch."

"Oh."

I could do magic. That was kind of awesome—and fortunate. Nerissa hadn't said anything about me needing to use magic to activate that device. What if I hadn't been able to do it? What if I'd passed through that barrier thinking I was protected, and it had burnt me alive? The good doctor and I would be having a little chat when I got back to the Legion.

"Oh, this is amazing. I've been wanting to share magic with you forever, and now I can," Bella told me, glowing with excitement. "I'm going to give you a list of my favorite spells."

I nodded, secretly wondering how long it would take me to get through the fifty million other books Nero had put on my reading list.

"Do you know where they keep the inventory records up here?" I asked her.

"They make us write out all of our records by hand, but I believe the professors' own records are kept here." She tapped the computer sitting on the desk in the corner.

"Can you get me a copy of all records mentioning Sunset Pollen or Snapdragon Venom?"

"Magitech isn't my specialty, but I'll see what I can do," she said, sitting at the desk. Her fingers flew over the keys. For someone who claimed not to be good at tech, my sister certainly was a typing fiend. "Leda?"

I glanced up from the cabinet I was looking through. "Yeah?"

"Do you really think the witches here are behind poisoning all those people?"

"Morgana is the head of the Chemistry department at the only place in the world that makes the two poisons. And it looks like she used the venom from Constantine's animals to make them." The two of them were looking really guilty at the moment.

"Morgana I could believe. She is…intense," Bella

decided. "Brilliant and powerful, but also a little crazy. But I don't think Constantine would help her kill so many people. He values all life, whether human or supernatural or animal. Before we dissect an animal, he speaks a quick prayer for their soul."

"That doesn't mean he's not in on this. It's the good ones you have to watch out for the most. When they fall, they fall hard."

Bella glanced back at me. "When did you become so cynical?"

"I've always been cynical, or at least a part of me has been. That's the part that was a huge asset when I was a bounty hunter. It helped me think like the people we were chasing, which in turn helped me catch them. I try to only let that part of me out when I'm working. Miss Cynic can be a real party pooper."

"I'll bet." Bella's gaze returned to the computer screen. "Weren't the victims in the Brick Palace all vampires?"

"Yes, they were. I didn't even know you could poison vampires."

"You can with those two poisons," she said. "Morgana's team designed them to work against supernaturals."

"Which supernaturals?"

"All of them."

"But not soldiers of the Legion."

"Ok, not all. But you're different. You've already been poisoned by something more potent than anything we can make on Earth."

"You're talking about Nectar," I said.

"Yes. What is the Nectar of the gods if not a poison designed to kill anyone who doesn't fit a specific set of criteria?"

"I guess I never thought about it that way." If Nectar

really was poison, then that meant I got a rush from drinking poison. And why did I get that same high from Nero's blood? Did that mean angel blood was poison too? This was all too bizarre for me to think about right now—or basically ever— so I chose blissful ignorance over enlightenment. There would always be time to be enlightened later, when I wasn't trying to save the city.

"Ok, if the soldiers of the Legion are immune to these poisons, that explains why someone tried to blow us up rather than poison us at lunch today. Or at least tried to scare us by making us think they were going to blow us up," I said.

"And you think this someone is the same person behind poisoning the vampires?"

"At this point, Bella, I really doubt we're dealing with just one someone. The bomb in the dining room was Magitech."

"You can't believe Gwyneth is part of this too. She supports Aurora, not Morgana. She wouldn't help Morgana kill vampires."

"Maybe it's Aurora who's behind the attacks," I suggested.

"Why would Aurora use animal-based poisons? The Botany department has a few poisons that are just as deadly to supernaturals as those from the Zoology department."

"If it is Aurora, she might be trying to divert suspicion away from herself," I said. "I just don't know. None of this aligns. None of it makes sense. We're missing too many pieces to this puzzle."

"Well, I hope this will help you close the gap a bit." Bella handed me a tiny metal stick. "I copied over any file that references either Sunset Pollen or Snapdragon Venom."

I tucked the stick into my pocket. "Thanks. Now let's see what's brewing in the Zoology lab next door."

We walked toward the door, but before we made it there,

I heard voices echoing down the hall. I reached out and grabbed Bella's arm, stopping her.

"What is it?" she asked.

"Someone's coming."

Bella's eyes flickered to the ceiling. "Up there. We can hide in the crawl space."

Nero would *never* have approved of hiding. He'd have called it unbecoming of a soldier of the Legion. Well, he wasn't here, so he didn't get to have an opinion. The witches couldn't do anything to me—well, except maybe try to blow me up again—but they could expel Bella if they found her in the school's restricted corridor. I was not going to let that happen. If I'd been thinking straight, I never would have dragged her into this. I'd been too eager to solve the mystery, too willing to take risks.

I grabbed a broom and used it to push aside the ceiling panel. Then I helped Bella up into the hollow space above the ceiling. I followed her inside and settled the panel back into place. Through the cracks between panels, we watched the four leaders of New York's witch covens enter the lab.

"Why have you called us here at this late hour, Morgana?" Aurora demanded, tapping her foot against the floor.

"The Legion is keeping a close eye on us," her sister said to them all. If only she knew just how close we were. "Now more than ever, we must keep our hands clean."

"That isn't a problem for some of us," Gwyneth said with a cool look.

"Cute. Very cute," Morgana said. "But I know all about your dirty little project, Gwyneth."

"And I know about yours, Morgana," said Aurora. "I wonder what the Legion would have to say about it if they knew."

"If I burn, you burn, dear sister. Or do you think the Legion would turn a blind eye to what you've been doing?"

"Someone needs to explain to those two how sisters are supposed to treat each other," I whispered to Bella.

She squeezed my hand.

"No one is tattling to the Legion about anyone else," Constantine said. "There's no need to arouse their suspicion."

"The Legion is already here. And they are always suspicious," Aurora snapped at him.

"They are here because you two can't control your little spat," Gwyneth told the sisters. "Or your extracurricular activities."

Now we were getting somewhere. But before I could learn more about those extracurricular activities, a thick gas filled the lab. The witches moved faster than I'd guessed they could in their very stylish but completely impractical outfits. They fled the lab and hurried down the corridor, taking any chance I had of further eavesdropping along with them.

But eavesdropping was the least of our problems. The gas was leaking into our hiding space, and it didn't smell friendly.

"Poison," Bella coughed.

CHAPTER 14

PLAYING NINJA

I pushed open the ceiling panel. Thanks to the gods' first gift, I was immune to the noxious gas, but Bella was not—and she couldn't hold her breath indefinitely. We had to move quickly. Bella and I hopped down. I waved at her to run down the hall while I quickly set the panel into place.

Once it was back where it belonged, I ran down the hall after her. Hand-in-hand, we made it through the green barrier. I could hear footsteps rushing up the stairs. I pulled a black mask over my face and tucked my hair hastily inside. But Bella was completely exposed. If university security was coming, she'd get in trouble for being up here. I hurried to the window and pulled it open.

"Here." I handed her some rope. "We'll use this to scale down the building."

"No need for that," she replied with a smile.

She slid a vial out of her skirt pocket. As soon as she pulled out the stopper, a whirlwind whispered out of the top, surrounding us both. Encased in magic, we climbed onto the windowsill and jumped. The wind cushioned our fall the whole way down. Bella pushed the stopper back into place, and the spell dissipated.

"Cool," I said.

She winked at me. "Just wait until you see the new healing potions I can make."

"I'm afraid that will have to wait for another time," I told her. "You need to get out of here before someone sees you."

"Are you sure you'll be all right?"

"I can take care of myself."

She hugged me tightly. "I know you can."

She pulled away, giving me a little wave before turning to walk calmly down the paved path to Building 3, her movements so innocent that no one would possibly imagine that she'd been doing more than enjoying a late night stroll. At least I hoped no one would stop her. The only trouble Bella had ever gotten into in her life was entirely because of me. She didn't have a drop of wickedness in her.

I could sense people approaching, and from the way they were moving, *they* definitely weren't witches out for a late night stroll. Four very large men dressed in black strode out of the building we'd just escaped. I might have thought they were university security—if not for the masks they wore. As one, the masked assailants rushed me.

I sidestepped one of them, giving him an added push as he passed. He slammed into the brick building. The impact wasn't enough to knock him out, but it was enough to leave him dazed. The other three had surrounded me, hitting me with a coordinated punch. If they'd been vampires or shifters, that would have been game over for me, but despite their muscular appearance, the men weren't supernaturally strong. They weren't supernaturally fast either.

And I was both. I caught one man's arm and pulled him in front of me like a shield. It all happened so fast that his buddies' fists hammered into him instead of into me. The man dropped to the ground, unconscious. I looked down at him, hardly believing that had worked. The other two guys were gaping like they didn't believe it either.

Thick arms closed around me from behind, trapping me. It looked like the dazed man I'd pushed into the building had recovered. I stomped down hard on his foot. He grunted, and I kicked his shin. I followed that up by slamming my head back into his face. I hit him so hard that I knocked him out. These moves worked *so* much better when my opponent wasn't an angel.

I turned to face the last two guys. Floodlights flared up all across the grounds. I blinked rapidly, trying to clear my vision. Through the purple blotches swirling across my eyes, I saw the real university security rushing toward us. The two masked men still standing turned and ran, abandoning their unconscious comrades. Nice.

I ran too. Ideally, I would have grabbed one of the men off of the ground. Realistically, he looked far too heavy. Sure, I was strong, but I knew my limits, and carrying him was outside of them. I couldn't move fast enough with that extra weight—at least not fast enough to escape the security closing in on me from all sides. And even *without* the extra weight, I might not be able to escape. I briefly considered staying but dismissed the idea. To avoid being arrested, I'd have to tell them I was with the Legion, but I wasn't really supposed to be here, was I? If I got caught, Nero would find out that I'd broken into the university without his permission. I was really not in the mood to argue with him right now.

I detoured into Angel Park to strip down to my sport bra and running shorts. I quickly stuffed my overclothes into the small backpack I'd brought along, then continued running down the sidewalk. Now instead of a ninja, I looked like any other runner out for some late night exercise.

At the Legion, the night security guy at the desk was playing games on his computer. He hardly looked up at me as I passed. The halls were empty. Everyone must have been asleep—or still out partying. Back in our apartment, Ivy and Drake were sitting on the sofa, watching a cheesy martial arts movie.

"Hey, are you all right?" Ivy asked, pausing the movie. "I was worried after you rushed out of Three Wishes."

I plopped down on the sofa next to her. "I'm fine. I just infiltrated the witches' university, had someone try to kill me with poisonous gas, and fought masked assailants."

"Cool," Drake said.

"Cool?" Ivy rolled her eyes at him. "What exactly is cool about that?"

"She got to go on a secret Legion mission. That is cool."

"Actually, it was a secret Leda mission. The Legion knows nothing about it, and let's keep it that way." I dug the memory stick out of my bag. I'd have to come up with a story for how I'd gotten it. A story that didn't involve breaking into the university without Nero's permission.

"Colonel Windstriker doesn't know you went there?" Drake snorted. "That's going to be a fun conversation when he finds out."

"Not if he doesn't find out."

Drake gave me an indulgent smile. "Ok, Leda. He won't find out."

"Shit. He's going to find out," I said. Drake was right. Nero always found out about everything.

"Unless he's distracted," said Ivy, wiggling her eyebrows.

I ground my teeth. "You saw what happened at the club."

"Hard to miss that pink fairy all over him." She squeezed my hand. "I'm sorry, honey."

"Nero can kiss whoever he wants. I don't care." I rose from the sofa. "Playing ninja is exhausting. I'm going to bed now."

That night I dreamed that it had been me on that sofa with Nero in Three Wishes, and that we'd done a lot more than just kiss. He'd drunk from me, and I from him. I woke up the next morning drenched in sweat. I lifted my hand to my throat, where my pulse throbbed against my skin. I could almost still feel where he'd bitten me, and it hadn't even been real. It had been just a dream. I fell back onto the mattress with a heavy sigh. I was in so over my head with that angel.

CHAPTER 15

THE DOG HOUSE

*M*y dream had awoken me just a few minutes before my alarm clock went off, so there was no point in going back to sleep. I pulled on my training clothes, then headed down to the gym. I wasn't looking forward to seeing Nero again, but I couldn't just back out of our training sessions. I was getting better because of them, as last night's fight against the masked assailants had reminded me.

I could do this. I could train with Nero and not think about…well, anything but the training. I took a deep breath and opened the door to the gym. Nero was waiting for me inside, but he wasn't alone. Jace and Captain Somerset were standing beside him.

I was about to walk over to them when Nero said, "There's no need to disrupt your morning workout routine, Pandora. Fireswift will spot you."

Ok, all business it was. That was good. I walked over to the weight bench. The barbell was already loaded. I cursed under my breath at the weight Nero had loaded on. Either he'd forgotten to switch out his own weights, or he was punishing me for something. Since it felt like Nero was always punishing me for something, I was going with the latter.

"The inquisition team finished speaking with the witches we brought here for questioning," Captain Somerset said.

The inquisitors had questioned everyone in the school yesterday afternoon, but they'd invited a few special some-ones here for followup questions. Yes, 'invited' was the word they'd used, as though they were simply inviting them to tea. The Legion had a pretty dark sense of humor.

"No one knew anything," she said.

The Legion inquisitors were notoriously thorough. If they hadn't found anything, there either wasn't anything to be found, or someone had cast a spell on them that prevented them from revealing secrets under torture. But only a god or a demon had magic powerful enough to cast a spell that would withstand the Legion's inquisitors.

Nero seemed to be thinking along the same lines. "The supernaturals that the inquisitors questioned about their defection to the demon army also revealed nothing. If these witches have the same master, they may be under the same spell," he said as I lowered onto the workout bench.

"What do we do?" Captain Somerset asked him.

"If you use a strong enough hammer, eventually you can crack through anything," he replied.

I slid the bar off the stand and began to bench-press the weights Nero had given me. By the third repetition I was cursing his name. By the tenth, I was yearning for the power to set that evil angel on fire.

"Are you all right?" Jace asked me.

"Fine," I huffed, lifting the bar again.

"I can't believe you're lifting that. It's over three hundred pounds, and you're not a very big girl."

"Not…helping," I growled.

"People with supernatural powers require supernatural challenges," Nero said, watching me as I settled the bar back onto its stand.

I moved on to the next station, exercising my shoulder muscles. "It feels at least as good as it hurts just so long as you imagine yourself slamming the weights into the source of your supernatural suffering," I whispered to Jace.

He turned his back to our audience to hide the smile on his face. Nero continued to watch me as though I were a bomb that would explode at any moment.

"There is another matter to discuss," he told Captain Somerset. "There was an incident at the New York University of Witchcraft last night. One involving someone dressed as a ninja."

I nearly dropped my weights. I steadied my grip just in time.

Captain Somerset snorted. "A ninja? A bit early for Halloween, isn't it?"

"University security chased the ninja off the campus, but they were too slow. Or, more accurately, the ninja was too fast," Nero continued, staring at me.

Yeah, he knew who the ninja had been all right. Why did I even bother? Drake was right. You couldn't hide anything from Nero. He always found out.

"Did they catch the four masked men?" I asked casually, beginning my bench dips. I had to do a few hundred of them to feel the burn.

"Yes. They were not as fast as the ninja." His eyes narrowed. "I don't remember assigning you to break into the witches' university last night."

"Oh, really?" I laughed. "Well, you were so *distracted* that I guess you must have forgotten all about it."

Captain Somerset swallowed a shocked chortle. I didn't even know what had compelled me to say that, but I wasn't going to back down now. I'd already jumped in with both feet. So I met Nero's stare with foolish determination.

"What did you find out at the school?" he asked. His face could have been carved from granite for all the emotion it was showing right now. It was no wonder sculptors liked to make statues out of angels. They were practically statues already.

"The four department heads met in a lab protected behind a magic barrier," I said, surprised that he hadn't decided to punish me right then and there. Maybe my information was more appealing than the thought of torturing me. "They don't get along well from the sounds of their verbal warfare. I was just about to hear them spill all of one another's dirty secrets when poisonous gas flooded the lab, and they ran away."

"So, in other words, you risked exposing our investigation and disobeyed me, and you have nothing to show for it."

"I didn't disobey you," I argued. "You never forbade me from going there."

"You should have learned by now that pulling technicalities out of your ass won't save you."

Ripples of glee split across Captain Somerset's face. She sure was having fun.

"And it wasn't for nothing," I added. "I have a copy of every inventory list and lab report where Sunset Pollen or Snapdragon Venom is mentioned."

"Where is this copy?" he asked.

"Somewhere safe. If you ask nicely, I might even give it to you." I smirked at him. Well, if I was going to get punished anyway, I might as well earn it.

He met my smirk with perfect calmness. "It's in your underwear drawer."

"My underwear drawer is none of your business," I shot back, flushing. How on earth had he guessed that? I'd been blocking his mind-reading mojo. "Something weird is going on at that school." When backed into a corner, the best strategy was to just change the subject. "You need to put a tail on all four of the coven leaders."

"I know how to do my job, thank you," he replied coolly.

I glared back at him.

"Who let the blizzard in here?" Captain Somerset commented, shivering.

"You will hand over the records you procured last night," Nero continued. "Bring them to Dr. Harding in her lab. She is testing the samples we took from the explosion in the restaurant yesterday. You and Fireswift will spend the morning assisting her and her team."

I'd just finished my last round of exercises, so Jace and I left the gym hall. While he grabbed breakfast for us, I ran upstairs to get the memory stick. Then together we headed for Nerissa's lab.

Five hours later, we knew the bomb that tried to blow us to pieces yesterday had been made from components exclusive to the research division of the university's Steam department. I couldn't bring myself to be surprised. The question now wasn't whether the witches were behind all of this; it was *which* of the witches were behind it. How many of their dirty little projects were about to go off? I buried my head in my hands.

"You're stressed," Jace commented.

I looked up at him. "No, thinking for too long just makes my brain hurt."

"I have the perfect remedy."

"No time for Nectar now."

"No, not Nectar. Lunch."

"Good idea," I agreed immediately. "I heard Demeter is serving lasagna today."

"I'm talking about something much better than lasagna." He stood up. "Come on."

———

I LOOKED AROUND THE DINING AREA OF THE DOG House, restaurant by day, shifter party palace by night. The Dog House. I couldn't decide if the shifters were trying to be funny with that name or not.

"You're right. That was much better than lasagna," I told Jace as I licked the ketchup from my fingers. A hamburger wrapper, all that remained of my lunch, lay on the counter. The pleasure of meeting that burger's acquaintance had cost me twenty dollars, but it had been worth every cent. Shifters might have had testy temperaments, but they knew their meat.

"How could I not know this place existed?" I asked. "It's practically next door."

Jace chuckled. "Because you hardly ever venture out, Miss Work Ethic."

"Says the guy who's been training for the Legion his whole life."

"Yeah, well…" He shrugged. "I have a destiny to live up to, you know. Enemies to smite, friends to backstab."

I grabbed my milkshake and sucked in a slurp of chocolate heaven. "It doesn't have to be that way. You could choose to be…"

His brows lifted. "Not a brat?"

"The sort of person you want to be," I amended. "When

you're being yourself—not what you've been told to be—you're not all that bad, you know." I swiped a fry from his plate.

"You *must* like me if you're stealing my fries."

I dunked the fry into my shake. "Nah, I just like your fries."

He snorted. "You're not what people think you are."

"Oh, so I'm not a snarky, fry-stealing, rule-breaking rebel?"

"Ok, there is *that*," he said. "But you're more. You're nice. You don't hate people."

"Hating takes too much effort that could be spent on better things."

"My parents hate you," he told me.

"I don't believe I have ever met your parents."

"No, you haven't. But it's not really you they hate. It's what you represent."

"Anarchy?"

He snorted. "No, a threat to me. To my holy, preor-dained rise to ultimate power."

"Well, if it's really preordained, then I'm no threat to you, am I?" I pointed out. "And I'm no threat to you anyway."

"My father called me after they heard what happened at lunch yesterday." Something about his tone told me Colonel Fireswift hadn't called to express his relief that his son had survived. "He berated me for throwing myself on you when the bomb went off."

"Ah, I guess that I, as the more expendable of the two of us, was supposed to do the self-throwing."

"That's not it," he said. "He wasn't pleased that I'd helped my biggest competition."

"*I* am your biggest competition? Not the five other men and women who have an angel parent?"

"He warned me not to help them too much either. He wants me to be someone whose only friend is power."

"And what do you think about that?" I asked him.

"That that's a shitty way to live."

I lifted my milkshake. "To swearing off loneliness."

He clinked his glass against mine. "To telling my dad to piss off."

"No," I gasped, grinning. "You didn't."

"In a very respectful and polite way."

"You mouthed off to an angel." I giggled. "That is awesome."

"You mouth off to an angel every day."

"Yeah, but I'm not you. I have a problem keeping my mouth shut."

"Something I'm sure Colonel Windstriker will appreciate when he's kissing you."

My jaw dropped. "You did *not* just tease me."

"Did I do it wrong?" He gave me a sheepish look.

I burst into laughter. "No, you did it just fine." I patted him on the back.

"So, what is between you and Colonel Windstriker?"

"Nothing," I said. "Absolutely nothing."

"I see." He turned his gaze to the wall behind the bar. "So, what would he think of us eating lunch together."

I smirked at him. "What, you think this is a date?"

"No, just two friends having lunch. But I'm not sure he would see it in the same way."

"Nero doesn't hold any claim over me." He'd made his lack of feelings for me perfectly clear last night when he'd made out with that pink fairy. "So who cares what he thinks?"

"I do actually. He's even scarier than my father, and I

don't want to end up on the wrong end of his fury. Or his punishment."

"You get used to his punishments after a while. You only have to get worried if he sends you to Hall 10."

"What's in Hall 10?"

"Let's hope you never find out." I winked at him.

"You're messing with me."

"I'd never do such a thing." I looked around for the bartender. "Where is that man when you need him?"

"His shift is over. What can I get you, sweetness?"

I turned around to find Stash, the werewolf I'd arm-wrestled last night, behind me. As I met his eyes, golden swirled with the green inside his irises.

"Hey, great to see you!" I grinned at him. "You work here too?"

"On Saturday afternoons."

"Cool, then I'll have to come back again on a Saturday afternoon." I handed him my empty glass. "And I'll take another triple chocolate milkshake, please."

"Coming right up."

"You know a werewolf?" Jace whispered to me as Stash made my shake.

"Sure, Stash and I go way back to last night when I defeated him in a round of armwrestling."

"Speak a bit louder, sweetness." Stash set my milkshake down on the counter. "I don't think the weretiger in the back heard you."

I smiled sweetly at him over the top of my monster-sized shake. "That weretiger has been checking out your manly muscles since you stepped behind the bar. I don't think I could say anything that would change her opinion of you. In fact, I wouldn't be surprised if she soon decided she needed a milkshake too. Making them is so…active." I slid my tongue slowly across my lips.

As if on cue, the female weretiger dressed in a leather motorcycle suit rose from her seat.

"You are a wicked woman," Stash said in a low rumble.

"You're welcome."

The weretiger strutted over to the bar. She leaned her elbows on the counter, her back arching into a smooth curve as she pushed her chest forward and her butt back. Every eye in the place turned to gape, Jace included. I chuckled.

When I drew in breath again, I nearly choked on the foul stench in the air. I looked up to find smoke pouring out of the air vents, rolling across the ceiling like dark storm clouds.

"Poison," I told Jace. I jumped up onto the bar counter. "By the authority of the Legion of Angels, I order you all to get the hell out of here!" I shouted, surprised at how well my voice carried across the whole room.

I didn't have to ask twice. Whether thanks to their fear of the darkening cloud of poison or my evoking the Legion, every person in the bar ran for the exit. Jace and I waited to make sure everyone was gone, then we followed them.

"Call the Legion," I told Jace, then walked over to Stash. The rest of the shifters were looking to him for guidance. "Are you some kind of big deal in the shifter community?"

"I was once. Before my exile."

"It looks like you still are," I said. "I need you to use that fame to convince these people to stay put. Some of them don't look so great. They must have inhaled too much of the poison. I want our healers to take a look at them."

"We can heal ourselves," one of the shifters protested.

"Your hand is turning silver," I pointed out. "Whatever is in that gas, it doesn't care about your super-healing." She opened her mouth to speak, but I was faster. "You seem to think you have a choice. Now sit down, shut up, and wait for our healers to arrive."

"You were channeling Colonel Windstriker there," Jace said, coming up beside me.

I didn't respond to the quip. "When will the healers arrive?" I asked him.

"They'll be here in two minutes," Jace told me. "But we have a different problem."

"I see it."

We'd closed the door of the club to trap the poisonous gas inside, but it wasn't enough. Black smoke was oozing through every gap and crack in the building. And if we didn't find a way to stop it, these shifters wouldn't be the only lives the gas claimed. It would spread across the entire city.

CHAPTER 16

ANGEL'S KISS

I didn't have any clue how to contain the poisonous gas, but maybe I could make it change form. I'd read about switching-state spells in one of the books on witchcraft Nero had assigned me. Of course, books were one thing and real life was another. Just because I'd read about the spell, that didn't mean I could do it. But I had to try.

"Give me your Fire Salt and Sea Breeze," I said to Jace.

He pulled two vials out of his potions kit, one filled with tiny red crystals and one with fine blue sand. I poured them together onto my palm, willing their magic to mix. The combined mixture began to pop, tickling my skin. I tossed a handful at the nearest poison puff. Magic crackled, and the gas thickened into a thick, snot-like goo that dropped out of the air, smacking the pavement.

I poured and mixed and tossed, taking that cloud out, piece by piece. By the time the Legion containment crew arrived, neither Jace nor I had a single grain of Fire Salt or Sea Breeze left.

"You didn't leave anything for us," Nerissa said as the last clot of poisonous goo hit the ground.

"Sure, we did. Those people need your help." I pointed at the shifters. "They've been poisoned."

Nerissa waved the healers over to take care of the shifters. "That was quick thinking," she said, glancing down at the forest of goo that covered the sidewalk in front of the building. "How ever did you think of changing the poison from gas to solid to stop it from spreading?"

"I read it in a book."

I looked around. The healers were already taking care of the poisoned shifters. I glanced over as the silver sheen faded from their skin. That had been close. Whatever this poison was, it was designed to aggressively kill shifters. It was by luck alone that they'd all survived the attack.

First vampires, then us, and now shifters. The witches were targeting us one by one, and we still had no clue why. I knew it was the witches, just as I knew that when Nerissa analyzed the poison, she'd find it was yet another super-poison made only within the gilded gates of the New York University of Witchcraft.

I was tired—really tired. Igniting the magic in those potions had drained me of everything I had. I needed a nap, not another crime scene.

And I definitely don't need this, I thought as Nero came around the corner. He headed straight for me. I was so *not* in the mood to deal with him right now.

He stopped in front of me. "We need to talk." Then he turned and walked back the way he'd come.

I didn't have the energy to argue with him right now, so I followed him. Neither of us said a word the whole walk back to the Legion. The silence held until we stepped into his office and he closed the door behind us.

"Are you all right?" he asked me.

I didn't want to consider the consequences of him actually caring about me, so I brushed him off. "I'm fine."

"Stop," he said when I moved toward the door.

I pivoted around. "I just saw a lot of people nearly die. Do you have to punish me now?"

"Punish you? For what?"

"For last night. For sneaking around the witch university without your permission. You said you were going to punish me."

"Yes, I did say that."

"I'm really tired. Can't I just take the pushups later?" I pleaded.

"You just saved the lives of over fifty people. Let's call it even."

I blinked in surprise. "So you're not going to punish me?"

"I am not going to punish you," he confirmed.

"Oh. Good. So, then why am I here?"

"Because I need to talk to you."

"About what?"

"You are angry with me," he said.

"I'm not." I resisted the urge to cross my fingers behind my back.

Nero wasn't fooled. "Don't lie to me."

I sighed. "What do you want me to say?"

"Start with the truth."

I let out a strained laugh. "I don't think that would be a good idea." I began to turn away.

"We're not done."

"What is this all about?" I demanded. "Is it professional or personal?"

"Personal."

"Then I'm leaving. I don't want to talk to you right now."

"You forget your place." A warning note hummed at the surface of his words.

"No, you forget yours," I snapped. "This isn't how this works. You can't just order me to listen to you about whatever personal thing you want to get off your chest. I'm leaving." I turned to leave, but his hand closed around my wrist. "Let go."

"Leda."

"Oh, no. No, no, no. You can't just 'Leda' me and then everything is all better." I tried to shake him off, but the man had an iron grip. "Let me go, Nero," I bit out.

"Talk to me."

He looked irked at being denied what he wanted. Good. I was pissed as hell at him right now. He couldn't just hold me here. I would have swung a punch at his perfect, obnoxious face except I wasn't even allowed to hit him. That would get me into trouble. I unclenched my fist.

He realized what I was thinking—or he'd just read my thoughts. "I absolve you from any repercussions of hitting me."

He didn't have to say it twice. I swung a punch at him—a fast, hard punch. He caught my fist in his hand.

"If you can hit me," he added.

The arrogant bastard. I tried to hit him again, but he was too fast. He was always too fast. It was one of his most annoying qualities, especially right now. Would it kill him to stand still and let me get in a punch? I growled in frustration.

"Are you done yet?" he asked with infuriating calmness.

"Not even close." I aimed for his head, and he captured my other hand. "I'm just waiting for the right opening."

"Take your time."

"You…" I pushed against his hand. "…are…" I made a

futile attempt to kick his shin. "…so…" Futile or not, I tried again—and failed. "…aggravating." I growled at him.

"So I've been told."

I couldn't help but laugh. It was a hard, tortured laugh. "When are you going to let me go?"

"After we've talked about what is going on between us."

"There is nothing going on between us. Nothing. You made that perfectly clear last night."

"Last night was a mistake."

"This whole thing was a mistake. You. Me. Me thinking we could…" An angry noise buzzed in my mouth.

"We could what?" he said quietly.

"It doesn't matter. This could never work."

"Last night was a mistake," he repeated. "Basanti found the fairies. They were so excited to go on a double date with two soldiers of the Legion of Angels."

Why the hell was he telling me this?

"All of us have a little of the vampire in us, Leda. We don't have to drink blood to survive, but that doesn't mean the hunger doesn't hit us too. Lately, I've been feeling this hunger, this growing hunger. Basanti told me I'm too wound up, that I need to relax."

"You don't have to explain yourself to me. You don't owe me anything," I said. "In fact, don't. I don't want to hear about it."

"I'm wound up because of you," he told me, his thumb rubbing the inside of my wrist, tracing circles across my veins.

I closed my eyes. "I can't listen to this."

"I couldn't."

"You couldn't what?" I asked, opening my eyes.

"Act on that hunger last night. Because it wasn't for that fairy. It was for you."

I felt the fight in me go out like a light. My muscles went liquid.

"When I saw you there, the pain in your eyes, the jealousy—"

"Thinking a bit highly of yourself, are you?"

"You aren't the only one," he told me. "Jealousy is a merciless fiend."

"Kind of like an angel," I muttered.

"When I saw you leave the office for lunch with Fireswift, I nearly intervened."

Translation: he'd nearly lost it and attacked Jace. I could see a hint of that madness burning in his eyes now.

"Jace is just a friend."

"Friends with a Legion brat?" He leaned in, his mouth spreading into a smile so delicious I could hardly resist the temptation to steal a taste.

"Yes, friends. You should try it sometime."

"Being your friend?"

"It sure beats being enemies."

He moved forward, and the room suddenly felt very small. "You shouldn't have been there with Fireswift. You should have been there with me."

I backed away. "You aren't interested in going out to lunch with me."

"No, the things I want to do to you cannot be done in public." His mouth dipped to kiss the underside of my wrist. Heat cascaded through my body like a burning river, searing everything it touched. "You don't know what you've done to me, Leda."

My retreat came to an abrupt end when the back of my legs bumped against his desk. In that moment, my mind flashed back to the last time we'd been alone in his office. I'd tossed my panties at his feet. His eyes flickered down to my legs. A slow, sexy smile spread across his lips, as though he were remembering it too.

"I'm not so easy," I said in clear contradiction to that memory.

"You want me."

"No." My body betrayed me, negating my denial.

"Look me in the eye and tell me that you honestly don't want me, then I will leave." His mouth quirked. "I won't even handcuff you to my desk this time."

Trying to calm the rush of heat in my cheeks—and everywhere else—I met his eyes. "Nero, I don't…" The words died on my tongue as soon as I saw my own longing reflected in his eyes. A hard, cruel ache twisted inside of me. "I can't." I slouched in defeat.

He lowered his mouth dangerously close to mine. "I thought not." His breath melted against my lips.

"Yes, I want you. But that doesn't mean we should—"

His mouth came down hard and heavy on mine, drowning my protest. His tongue slipped past my lips, ravaging the inside of my mouth with a hunger that was as delicious as it was deadly. The taste of him shot a sudden, merciless wave of pleasure through me that made my knees collapse out from under me. His hands lowered to my hips, catching my fall.

"Wait," I said, stopping his hand before it wandered lower.

He pulled back, but only far enough to tease me with the absence of his lips. All I wanted was to pull him against me and lose myself in this moment.

"Nero," I said slowly. If I moved my lips too much, they would touch his. If that happened, I wouldn't be able to resist kissing him again—and once *that* happened, I wouldn't be able to stop. "Yes, I want you.

But I don't want to be just another of your thousands of lovers."

"What are you talking about?" He didn't bother to keep his lips still. Every brush of them against mine was pure agony.

"Captain Somerset told me of your history," I said.

"She exaggerated."

"About you breaking their hearts?"

"About how many there were. It certainly wasn't thousands."

The perfectly casual way that he said it made my heart sink to my stomach. "Nero, I can't."

"Why not?"

"Because I'm not like you. I can't just be intimate with someone and not feel something. And I can't afford to feel for you, to have my heart broken. I have to save my brother. I have to worry about gaining the magic I need to find him. And if we do this, you *will* break my heart. Not today perhaps, but it will happen. You are an angel. And I am... I don't even know what I am anymore. But I feel mortal. I feel human. You would grow bored of me and my pesky humanity. And then that would be it. So I have to end this before that happens, before this is tearing me up even more than it already is."

I kissed him once softly on his lips, then I slid off his desk and hurried toward the door. And this time, he didn't try to stop me.

CHAPTER 17

BREAKING BOUNDARIES

They were serving pizza at Demeter tonight, but I skipped straight to dessert. There was nothing like a triple brownie sundae to get your mind off of witches, mass poisonings, and angels. I couldn't do anything about any of those things, but I *could* conquer this mountain of chocolate. Licking the syrup off my spoon, I stole a quick glance at the head table. Yeah, I was a sucker for punishment.

Nero had vacated his seat for Nyx. Nearly everyone in the canteen was staring at her—while trying to pretend that they weren't staring at her. I couldn't really blame them. Not only was Nyx a drop-dead gorgeous supernatural version of Snow White, she was the First Angel, and it wasn't every day that the First Angel came to dinner.

Nero sat to her right. When my eyes slid to him, he turned his head to look back at me. I hastily returned my gaze to my dessert. Chocolate was always safer than angels.

"Hey, Colonel Sexy Pants is looking at you," Ivy whispered to me.

"Does he look upset?"

"No, more like perplexed. He has this cute little crinkle

between his eyes, so adorably confused. That's a new look for him."

"I guess I defy his understanding of the world."

She chuckled and took a bite out of her pizza. Ivy ate even more than I did, and she still looked like a supermodel. She must have burned a lot of calories being awesome.

"Leda, you excel at defying boundaries," Drake said. His arm was wrapped around our former roommate Lucy. Those two sure were getting cozy.

I shrugged. "Why merely defy boundaries when you can break them down with a wrecking ball?"

"Who's the wrecking ball?" Lucy asked.

"Leda is the wrecking ball," Ivy told her, then glanced back at me. "Are you going out with us to Bloodfire tonight?"

"I don't know, Ivy. After how spectacularly last night ended, I'm not sure I want to go out again."

"Are you referring to Three Wishes or to your little field trip to the witch university?"

"Both. I think I'll stay in tonight and try to make a dent in that mountain of books beside my bed."

"How studious of you."

I grinned at her. "I know, isn't it? Wow, I think I'm cured. I'm a good girl now. I always behave myself and never, ever talk back."

"There will be a parade of fifty dancing angels the day that happens," Soren said as he walked up to our table. He dipped his head to kiss Ivy on the lips.

"I'm not that bad," I protested.

He gave me a hard look. I smirked back at him.

"You're cool, Leda," he said with a chuckle, then returned his attention to Ivy. "Ready to go?"

"Absolutely." Ivy stood and took his hand. "Are you sure

you won't come with us?" she asked me as Drake and Lucy rose too.

"I'm sure. Have fun."

"Ok, if you change your mind, you know where to find us," Ivy said.

Then she and Soren walked away, hand-in-hand, followed by Drake and Lucy, also hand-in-hand. I looked around the room. There sure were an awful lot of couples here. I supposed it was only natural. We lived and worked together at the Legion. It was inevitable that couples formed. People needed companionship.

Other people. Not you, I told myself as I went to go put my dinner tray away. I didn't need to play love roulette right now. I didn't want it.

Challenging that statement, Nero was suddenly beside me. My heart stuttered a surprised beat in my chest.

"You really have to stop doing that," I told him. "It freaks me out."

"If you were more aware of your surroundings, you wouldn't be surprised," he said. His tone was so cool, so professional, that I almost wondered if I'd imagined that whole scene in his office earlier.

"No matter how aware I am of my surroundings, I have a feeling I still wouldn't sense you unless you wanted me to," I replied with equal coolness.

"Yes."

I nearly laughed at the cold certainty of that single word, but the look in his eyes stopped me. His tone might have held no emotion, but his eyes burned with fiery intensity. I didn't know what I saw in those eyes, but it scared me.

"I have a job for you and Fireswift," Nero said, waving Jace over. "You will read through the records of all the witches the Legion captured last month, the ones who joined the demons' army. I want you to look for any connections between those witches, anything they have in common. If we can find a common link between them all, we might be able to determine which other witches are still free and doing the demons' bidding. And that will lead us to the witches behind the string of recent attacks on the supernatural community."

———

AFTER HIS JEALOUS SPEECH EARLIER, I WAS SURPRISED that Nero had assigned Jace and me to work together again. But then again, maybe it hadn't been jealousy. Maybe it had been just angel possessiveness at work. Or maybe he was simply a professional soldier and could separate his feelings from his work. Assuming he really did have feelings. He'd told me many times before that he couldn't afford them.

Jace and I had been sitting in the library for over four hours, reading through the Legion's files on the nine witches we'd captured in the Wicked Wilds last month, looking for connections that weren't there, grasping at straws that slipped through our fingers.

"Let's go through this one last time, and if we have no new brilliant insights, we can call it a night. What do you think?" I asked him.

"That I wanted to call it a night three hours ago," he said with a heavy sigh. He sat up straighter and rubbed his hands together to wake them up. "Ok, let's do this." He glanced down at our notes. "Are the nine witches from the same coven? The answer is no. The nine witches represent six different covens, some of them not even based in New York." He slid the sheet of paper over to me.

"Did the witches go to school together?" I read. "No, their educational backgrounds are all over the place too. We decided that those nine men and women seemed to share absolutely nothing in common with one another except for their desperation. The reasons for their hopeless situations are all different, but it was that feeling that led them all to the same place: into the demons' service."

"In other words, we know nothing," Jace summarized. "Colonel Windstriker won't be happy."

"Well, he'll just have to deal with it. We can't turn straw into gold. If there is nothing there, then there is nothing there. Glaring at us won't change the facts. Those witches had nothing in common… Wait, maybe we're going about this in the wrong way."

"What do you mean?"

"We were trying to find a connection between the witches."

"Because that's what Colonel Windstriker told us to do," Jace reminded me.

"I know, but I think we need to look at the attacks instead."

"The victims of the recent attacks—the vampires, us, and the shifters—have nothing in common either," he replied.

"Well, we are all supernaturals."

"So is a third of the population of New York."

"They are supernaturals, and they were attacked by supernatural means," I said. "More specifically, by witchcraft. The attacks themselves were all clearly the work of witches. The vampires' were killed by animal venom. The attempt to blow us up was powered by Magitech. And the black cloud that tried to kill the shifters came from plant poisons. The specific venom, Magitech, and poison are all experimental new spells found in only one place: the New York University of Witchcraft. The witches are in this so deep, you can read the writing on the wall."

"But we knew that already. This just brings us back to the witches, and we can't find anything they have in common."

"We couldn't find anything the nine witches in Legion custody have in common with each other, or anything that links them to the four New York coven leaders," I said. "But what if the two groups of witches aren't connected at all? What if the witches behind the recent attacks aren't working for the demons?"

"Each attack used magic from a different department, a different coven," he said. "And since the coven leaders don't get along with one another especially well, I think we can rule out the possibility of them all working together."

"Maybe two covens are working together, but not all of them," I agreed. "Morgana and Constantine are allies at the moment, and so are Aurora and Gwyneth. One of those allied pairs might be behind this, and they could have stolen supplies from the others."

"But why attack vampires and shifters? And you'd have to be crazy to attack soldiers of the Legion," Jace said.

"Whoever is behind this killed almost a hundred people, and they very nearly succeeded in killing even more. They *are* crazy."

"If the witch covens don't even get along with one another, then you'd think whoever is behind this would have attacked witches, not other supernaturals."

"I don't know. Maybe the supernaturals they attacked were helping their enemies?" I suggested. "I think that instead of pulling our hair out trying to figure out what links the witches, we should concentrate on what links the victims."

"To do that, we need records on all the victims."

"Yeah, which means we'll have to continue this tomorrow," I said.

"Thank the gods."

I chuckled. "Hey, do you want to stop by Nero's office and ask him for the records?"

"I think he'd prefer if you stopped by instead," he said. "Colonel Windstriker was giving me a look earlier."

"Define this look."

"A look that said he was going to set me on fire if I stepped out of line."

I thought back to Harker and how he'd set all those vampires on fire. Nero's magic was even more powerful.

"Ok," I said. "So he could set you on fire, but he won't. Don't worry about it. Nero *always* has that look. I just ignore it. Besides, you don't have anything to worry about. You never step out of line. You're the perfect soldier."

"You don't understand. This isn't about being the perfect soldier. This is about him thinking I'm trying to make a move on you. And it's about the consequences I'm going to face."

"Were you planning on making a move on me?" I smirked at him.

"No. But I don't think it matters to him. Paranoia and jealousy don't mix."

"Jace, he's not going to set you on fire for talking to me."

"I'm not too sure about that. That angel has it bad for you."

"He only wants me because I turned him down."

Jace snorted. "You turned down an angel? You're even crazier than I thought."

I shrugged. "Sanity is overrated."

"Leda," he said seriously. "No one who knows what's good for them says no to an angel."

"Then I guess I don't know what's good for me."

"Yeah," he laughed. "But you do realize that rejecting

him only made him more determined. That's how angels are. Trust me. I know. That's how my mom got my dad. He chased her for years, and for years she turned him down, which made him even more determined to have her. And once he finally got her, he wouldn't let her go. He worships the ground she walks on, just as she'd planned."

"Well, I'm not trying to 'get' Nero."

Quite the contrary actually. I was trying to forget all about him. I just wanted him to leave me alone—if only my body would get the message. But no matter how many times my mind told my body to stay cool, as soon as Nero was nearby, every cell in me went hyper alert, like I'd been hit by lightning.

"Just watch out, ok?" Jace said. "Angels are very possessive."

"I don't plan on being possessed."

"The way he's acting… You must have led him on somehow."

How about biting him and tearing his clothes off after I drank the Nectar to receive the gods' first gift? And thinking about doing that and more every single day? Gods, I *had* led him on.

"I'm not that interesting. He'll grow bored of chasing me eventually," I said.

"Ok," Jace replied, obviously not convinced. "I'm going to meet up with Mira and Kinley now. You want to come?"

"I don't think your other friends are ready to stop hating me yet."

"Give them time." He set his hand on my shoulder. "You can get the victims' records from the Colonel, right?"

"Well, since you're too chicken to go see him, I guess I have to," I grumbled.

"You're awesome," he said, grinning.

"Why is it people always flatter me when they want me to do something?" I demanded.

He left the room, chuckles trailing behind him. I gathered up all of the papers we'd spread across the table, then left the library, heading for Nero's office. He was probably still there—well, unless he'd found another eager and willing fairy to make out with him. Bah, who cared? I hurried down the corridor, determined to get this over with so I could get back to my room and that tower of textbooks waiting for me. Voices poured out of Nero's open office door, freezing me in my tracks.

"Colonel Fireswift wants to interrogate the four coven leaders," Nyx said.

"I'm sure he does," replied Nero gruffly.

"Colonel, this situation is getting out of hand. The Legion of Angels must always be in complete control. And right now, you aren't. People's fear of punishment is the only way we keep order. As soon as people think they can get away with something, they will grow bold. Every day, there's a new attack. If you don't put an end to them, I will give Colonel Fireswift his wish."

"Understood."

"Good, now I want to talk to you about Leda Pierce."

$\mathcal{M}$y breath caught when I heard Nyx speak my name.

"I like Leda," she told Nero. "And I see you share my appreciation."

"She is a competent soldier, though unorthodox," he replied. Wow, that was high praise from him.

"I see the way you look at her, Nero. You need to get yourself under control. Take her to your bed and be done with it. This is just making you agitated."

He said nothing.

Nyx chuckled softly. "You tried that already, didn't you? And she turned you down."

"Yes." He didn't sound like he shared her amusement.

"Well, try something else," Nyx said without sympathy. "Not everyone goes all wide-eyed and falls on their back for us."

"She is resistant."

Which was just another word for stubborn. A nicer word. Why was he never this nice when talking to me? Why did he have to always be such a hard ass?

"Have you tried compelling her?" Nyx asked him.

"Yes. It doesn't work on her. She's immune."

"Are you sure?"

"Positive. If she weren't, I'd have been able to make her stop mouthing off long ago."

Nyx laughed. "Perfect. Not since the early years of the Legion have we had someone join who possesses a natural immunity to an angel's compulsion."

If this immunity was so rare, that explained why Nero had looked surprised all those times I didn't fall under his spell like everyone else.

"I remember how your immunity used to annoy me," Nyx said to my surprise.

But I shouldn't have been surprised. Nero was insanely powerful, and he was even more stubborn than I was.

"This resilience makes her a valuable soldier," Nyx continued. "I see you've been training her extra. Good. She has the makings of a great angel."

"Yes."

"The two of you have something else in common. I saw how she reacted to the Nectar. You are the only other person who ever had that reaction. It makes me wonder… What do you know about her parents?"

"Nothing. She's an orphan. She doesn't remember them."

"Someone with that kind of power doesn't just drop out of the sky. It's in her blood," said Nyx. "Help her get through the Legion. We will need soldiers like her in the days to come. Things are about to get interesting."

"The demons."

"And so much more," Nyx said in the unnecessarily cryptic style I'd come to expect from angels. "But we have more immediate problems at the moment. Get this mess with the witches solved and settled, Colonel. I'd hate to execute them all."

I withdrew, hiding behind the door, holding my breath as Nyx passed out of Nero's office. I watched her stride down the corridor, her steps strong, her demeanor confident in the knowledge that she owned this place and everyone in it. Nyx was a delightfully odd combination of sweetness, beauty, humor—and hard, cruel angel.

I turned to peer through the door. Nero was sitting at his desk. Even though I'd just learned that he was two hundred years old, he looked so young right now, so forlorn. Like he didn't know what to do. Driven by this intensely human need to comfort him, I walked into his office.

"What is it, Pandora?" he asked, looking up at me. That lost boy was gone. The hard, calculating, perfectly-in-control angel was back.

"We couldn't find any connections between the witches," I said. "But we thought if we could get the backgrounds on the victims, we might find something there."

"I will have the files prepared and sent over to you."

"Ok." I squeezed my hands together, then realized how nervous that made me look. So I tucked them behind my back. "Great." I gave him a hesitant smile.

"Is there anything else?" he asked.

"No. I'll just be going then."

Nero's phone rang, and he picked it up. As he listened, I turned and walked away.

"I'll be right there," he said into the phone. I heard it clink against the receiver, then the sound of him pushing back his chair. "Wait."

I glanced over my shoulder to watch him strap on an extra belt of knives. "There's just been a break-in at the New

York University of Witchcraft. And an explosion that destroyed part of one building."

I whipped all the way around to face him. "Gods," I gasped. "Is everyone all right?"

"No one was killed. Your sister Bella is one of the witches caring for the wounded."

"That's so like her," I said, sighing in relief.

"The thief broke into the second floor of Building 2."

That's the same corridor Bella and I had snuck into. "What did the thief take?"

"Poisons, venoms, and explosives." He pulled on another belt of knives. "And this wasn't the university's first break-in. Apparently, their supplies have been going missing for weeks. They didn't want to admit to it because they were already under our scrutiny. They feared what would happen if we learned they'd lost so many deadly magics. This time, the thief triggered an alarm. The witches have upgraded their security since last night. The thief was trapped and had to blast his way out."

"Who is the thief?"

"They don't know. They suspect it is one of their own. They don't believe anyone but a powerful witch could have broken through the barrier protecting the second floor corridor."

"Which witch called to report this?" I asked.

"Morgana."

"She could be playing us."

"Yes, she could be," he agreed. "Which is why I'm not going to the university to talk to her and the other coven leaders. I'm sending Basanti instead."

"Where are you going?"

"I'm going to hunt down the thief. And you're coming with me," he told me.

"Me? Why me?"

"Because no one has been able to track the thief, and finding people is your specialty."

————

THE THIEF WASN'T STUPID. THE FACT THAT WE COULDN'T find him on any of the video feeds told me he knew where all the street cameras were. And he must have used a potion to cover his retreat because Nero couldn't find a trail—magical or physical—to follow. But that was ok. Back when I'd been a bounty hunter on the Frontier of civilization, I'd had neither video feeds nor the Legion's extensive arsenal of magic to help me. It was time to go back to basics.

Avarice was one of humanity's greatest failings, but I chose to see it as one of my most useful tools. A bundle of hundred-dollar bills went a long way in tracking a criminal, even on the relatively prosperous streets of New York. Within fifteen minutes, we'd followed the thief's trail from one helpful bystander to another. The money I offered them kept them talking, and the sight of the angel beside me kept them from lying to my face. That was efficiency at its peak, so Nero should have been happy. Instead, he looked like he'd soiled his shiny angel halo just by watching me bribe the local population.

"Stop it," I said as we hurried toward the Sunken Ship. The last guy we'd spoken to had told us we'd find the 'flying ninja' in an old warehouse by that name.

"Stop what?" Nero asked.

"Stop giving off that disgusted expression like something stinky died inside of your nose."

"I am giving off no such expression."

"You don't approve of my methods."

"You are stuffing hundred-dollar bills into the hands of strangers. It is…"

"Unseemly?" I suggested, arching my brows.

"Yes. A soldier of the Legion does not stoop to bribery."

"You asked for my help, and this is what it is. Your one thousand dignified soldiers of the Legion were unable to find the thief. Sometimes, the dignified way doesn't work. Sometimes, you just have to get your hands dirty."

"It remains to be seen whether anything at all will come of us getting our hands dirty."

"Oh, something always comes of it," I said, grinning. "It's just not always what you expected. Embrace the unexpected, Colonel. It's what makes life worth living."

"You are a very unusual woman."

"Thank you."

I stopped in front of a faded wooden sign with the words 'The Sunken Ship' painted across its uneven surface. The warehouse past the sign was in even worse shape. The roof was gone, and only three of the four walls were still standing. I could see into the hollow building, and it was empty.

"Not what you expected?" Nero asked me.

"No." My eyes traced the broken edges of the rotting building, up an elevator shaft to a raised platform. About the size of my living room, the platform was completely enclosed in glass. "I don't think the Sunken Ship is a warehouse." I tilted my head back further to gaze up into the sky. A crimson and bronze silhouette floated in front of the bright, full moon. "I think it's an airship."

CHAPTER 19

THE SUNKEN SHIP

A quick glance at the timetable posted to the wall of the decaying warehouse told me my guess had been right on the money. The Sunken Ship was an all-night floating party over New York City, and we'd just missed the final boarding call. We were stuck down here on the ground while the thief was up there now, plotting something evil.

"We have to find a way up there," I told Nero. "Before the thief blows that ship out of the sky. Or poisons everyone on board." I swallowed hard. "Or both. Maybe we can get a helicopter and—"

"Leda."

I turned to look at him. "What?"

"I am an angel. I can fly us up there."

"Both of us?"

"I can lift considerably more than your body weight."

"Oh, right," I said, suddenly feeling stupid.

He stepped in closer. "Put your arms around me."

As I looped my hands around his shoulders, his hands settled on my hips. In that instant, I flipped from feeling mildly stupid to feeling really self-conscious. Magic crackled in the air, and Nero's wings spread out from his body. Every time I saw that gorgeous blend of black, green, and blue feathers, my breath froze in my chest for a moment, as though my body wanted to freeze time, to give me just one moment to truly appreciate the exquisite perfection of his wings.

Nero bent his knees, then shot up into the air like a rocket. A moment later, we were high over the city, his wings pushing us toward the airship in hard, powerful strokes. We were moving fast—really fast. The night air slid across my face, moving down my body in cool rivulets. I shivered.

"You're cold," Nero said.

"No, I'm flying," I said, grinning. "This is just… I don't even know what words could describe it."

His eyes flickered to me. "You feel like it is the most natural thing in the world. You feel like before this moment, some part of you was incomplete."

"Yes, exactly that. How did you know?"

"Because I felt the same way the first time I flew." He turned his gaze forward. "We're almost there. Brace yourself."

"For what?"

Our feet slammed against the side of the airship so hard that the impact shot vibrations from my feet all the way up to my head. Nero's arms remained locked around me, which was a good thing because we were standing parallel to a several-hundred-foot drop into New York City. Only Nero's wings were keeping us in place.

"We will enter there," he said, pointing to a hatch in the airship's bronze hull.

It didn't appear openable from the outside, but that didn't stop Nero. He waved his hand, and the hatch flung open so hard that it ripped off its hinges. Nero caught the broken door as it flew past us.

"You used too much power," I told him.

"That was unexpected," he commented, glancing at the door in his hand. "They're usually attached better."

"So you do this often?" I said with a smirk as we moved into the airship.

"On occasion." He stepped away from me to get a closer look at the spot where the hatch had been mounted just a minute ago. "We are not the first to sneak aboard tonight. They burned their way through, then tried to staple the hatch into place." He lifted the door to the hole.

"And now you're going to do the same?" I asked him.

In response, he lifted up his free hand. Flames burst out of his palm. It took him half a minute to seal the hole in the airship.

"You welded the hatch shut," I said, gaping at his handiwork.

"Yes."

"But you *welded* the hatch shut," I repeated. "You melted through metal. I don't even know how hot your fire spell had to be to do that."

"Would you like me to answer that?"

"No." I tore my eyes away from the wall. "Let's just focus on finding our thief."

I walked down the hall toward the door at the end. Rising to my tiptoes, I peeked quickly through the circular window at the top. In the room beyond the door, a party was raging. Men and women dressed in a puzzling but not unpleasant contradiction of materials—ruffles and silk, leather and denim, metal and mesh—danced and drank and shared dignified laughs.

"This is a witch party ship," I whispered to Nero.

"Do you see the thief?"

"There are no ninjas dancing on the ceiling, but he probably changed clothes." I glanced back at him. "Even if he is in here, we wouldn't know it."

"I can."

"How?"

"The thief stole Ice Crystals."

"Another poison?" I asked.

"Yes, a potent one, so strong that it would have left an imprint on his aura. If we get close enough, I can sense that imprint, but we must hurry before it fades." He reached for the door handle.

I caught his hand. "Wait. We can't storm into the room dressed like this. We'll never get close enough to find the thief that way."

"I can freeze them with my mind."

"All one hundred people in that room?"

A crinkle formed between his eyes. "No, that's too many."

"Then it's a good thing I have a plan."

He gave me a wary look. "What kind of plan?"

"A fantastic one, of course."

———

I'D DONE JOBS ON A FEW PARTY AIRSHIPS BEFORE, AND they all had cabins for the guests to retire to when they needed to sleep off the drugs and fun. The abundance of cabins was good for us because we were going to borrow a new wardrobe. We had to break into three cabins before we had a complete ensemble for each of us. I tossed aside the leather jacket of my Legion uniform but kept the leather bustier I wore below it, as well as my leather boots. I paired them with black tights and a beige ballerina skirt.

"Take these," I told Nero, handing him a dark vest and a green dress shirt.

He gave them a hard look. "These clothes are ridiculous."

"Are you challenging the witches' sense of fashion?"

"Yes."

I chuckled and tossed him a belt with a wide buckle and funny symbols all over it. "Take that too. You can keep your pants on."

Silver swirled in his eyes for a brief moment before it faded into the green abyss. He held my gaze as he peeled the leather top off of his body. I didn't turn away. To do so would have been an admission that I was affected by the sight of his bare chest—by the hard, carved lines of muscle defined to delicious perfection by centuries of hard labor. Not that I was ogling either. Or drooling. Drooling would have given me away too.

Nero quickly pulled on the pilfered parts of his wardrobe. Then, dressed to kill, we walked out of the cabin, following the curving corridor back to the party zone. A soft, sweet ballad spilled out of the room when I opened the door. We navigated around a couple making out against the wall.

All of the interior walls were painted a cheerful shade of sunset. It matched beautifully with the midnight blue and gold of the night sky and city lights beyond the glass windows that encircled the room.

"How close do you need to be to pick up the Ice Crystal imprint?" I whispered to him as we zigzagged past ten people along our way to the bar.

"About three feet."

We circled around the bar, glancing down at the array of fancy appetizer platters sitting on the counter as we passed seven more witches.

"There are a lot of people here. This will take a while," I commented.

Nero held out his hand to me. "Dance with me."

"I thought you didn't dance," I said. "Or at least didn't dance with me."

In a moment of insanity, I'd once asked him to dance with me in a club. He'd turned me down. Weeks later, it still stung. The reasonable, logical part of me told me I shouldn't let it bother me, but I'd never been good at doing what I was told.

"There are thirty-two people on the dance floor. Dancing is the most effective way to get us close to all of them," he said.

"Oh. Ok."

So this wasn't really about dancing. Blushing, I took his hand, and he led me onto the dance floor. His skin burned against mine, like he had a fire raging inside of him.

"You're hot," I said.

His brows arched as he set his other hand on my back.

"I meant your temperature," I said quickly.

He shifted his weight in a firm but smooth movement that pivoted us around, moving us closer to another couple. "It's all the magic I've done tonight. It makes me hot."

I choked down a cough.

"I meant my temperature," he told me, his lower lip twitching.

I stared past his shoulder. "Another couple just stepped onto the dance floor. We haven't checked them out yet."

In response, he pivoted us again, moving us toward the new arrivals. From there, he led us past the others in a search pattern so methodical that I was surprised no one had noticed. Then again, no one came to a party expecting to be aura-scanned by an angel in disguise. And if the thief was here, he hadn't noticed either. I'd been tracking everyone in the room since we'd arrived, and no one had made a move to leave.

"I wanted to dance with you."

I paused my tracking for a moment to look at Nero. "What?"

"That time you asked me. I wanted to say yes."

My heart thundered. "What stopped you?"

"Everything."

I let out a pitiful laugh. I was trying not to feel anything, not to care, but it was hard when he was dancing so close to me, when his cheek was pressed against mine.

"I'm drawn to you, Leda," he whispered. His words kissed my ear, fluttering down my spine. "You are a drug— your blood, your magic, your very presence. And you make me human." He sighed. "I've tried to fight it, but it's no use. You consume my every thought. You invade my dreams."

I drew in closer, drinking in his words. He was my drug too, but that wasn't a solid foundation for a relationship. "If this is where you say let's just have sex so you can get me out of your system, then save your breath. I told you it doesn't work that way for me."

Nero's hand brushed softly down my cheek. "Leda," he said, his voice sensual, dark, ruthless. He spoke as though he knew he had me, and he was just waiting for me to finally realize it.

His eyes weren't cold now. They burned like an inferno. I knew that inferno would be the death of me, and the scary thing was I just didn't care. I wanted nothing more than to bathe in those flames with him.

I looked away from Nero before I did something stupid —and it was a good thing I had. "Two men are staring at us."

"Where?" he asked. Gone was the dark lover. Only the Legion soldier in him remained.

"By the bar."

Nero turned us around so he had a clear view of the bar. His eyes flickered to the men before returning to me. The movement was so quick that I barely caught it, and only because I was in front of him. Unless they had angel senses, they couldn't have seen it from across the room.

"The bald man is Pyralis Carver," he said to me.

"You know him?"

"He is Morgana Bennet's predecessor, the former leader of the Scimitar coven."

"Morgana overthrew him?" I asked.

"With the help of the other covens, yes."

"What is he doing here?"

"Nothing good," said Nero. "I don't recognize the man with him. Whoever he is, he doesn't belong here. He's no witch."

"What is he?"

"From the feel of his magic, a shifter."

"A werewolf?"

"Yes."

"You are getting all of this from his aura?" I asked.

"Yes."

"Let's move in closer to see what else you can sense from those two." Like Ice Crystals.

"No need. I will bring them to us."

He let go of me, striding forward. A tendril of electric-blue magic slid out of each of his hands. In a flash of speed, he cracked those magic whips, looping them around the mens' ankles. Nero heaved on the sizzling whips, and the men flew off their feet, hitting the wood floor with a hollow thump. He pulled again to bring them to rest in front of his feet. He looked down on them, his nostrils flaring as he inhaled deeply.

"You stole something that doesn't belong to you," he told the men.

Pyralis Carver's mouth twisted into a demented smile. "Now I'm going to give it back."

Everyone in the room dropped to the floor.

CHAPTER 20

BETWEEN HELL AND EARTH

*U*nlike the hundred witches who'd been partying just a few seconds ago, Nero and I were still standing. Pyralis Carver and his shapeshifting friend shot us a surprised look, then jumped up and ran, their footsteps thumping over the soft heartbeats of the sleeping witches. Thank goodness the partiers weren't dead.

Nero was already running after the assailants. Leaving the witches, I pushed through a side door and followed him into the underbelly of the airship. Dull, blinking lights illuminated our path down a very industrial-looking corridor. We passed exposed pipes screwed to the ceiling, and cables spilling out of holes in the walls.

The dark corridor ended in a storage bay. Six people dressed in black—plus Pyralis Carver and the shapeshifter dressed in the witch style—stood in a solid line blocking our path. As we ran through the door, thick steam shot out from either side of the frame, enveloping us. It burned my skin everywhere it touched. And in my current outfit, it touched a lot of places. I closed my eyes to shield them. Supernatural senses were a two-edged sword. Being ultra-sensitive wasn't always a good thing, particularly when flesh-burning gas was involved.

A shock wave of air shot out from beside me, blasting the gas away. The burning sensation on my skin faded, and I opened my eyes. Nero stood with his hands extended in front of him, the distinctive pale blue glow of air magic sparkling on his fingers. He was blinking hard, obviously trying to clear his vision. His senses were even more developed than mine—and even more sensitive. I tried to take a step forward, but my leg wouldn't move.

"It didn't work," said one of the women in black.

Pyralis Carver frowned. He pressed a button on the small remote in his hand. Steam billowed out of the doorframe, smothering us in that vile poison a second time. The burn was stronger this time, piling pain onto the first dose.

"They're supposed to be dead," the woman growled at him, gold light flashing across her brown irises. She was a shifter.

"A minor miscalculation."

"We're sick and tired of your 'minor miscalculations'." The woman looked at the men and women who'd clustered around her like she was their leader. They nodded, their eyes burning with that same gold light of shifter magic.

"If it were so easy to poison Legion soldiers, someone would have done it already," Carver said.

"You said you could do it."

"Enough." Nero's voice was hard, the golden gleam in his eyes rivaling their own. His hand shot up, and a psychic wave blasted the seven shifters and one witch across the room. Their backs slammed against the wall, where they remained stuck. "What are you doing on this ship?"

The panel beneath Nero's feet exploded, dousing him in a green liquid that immediately burst into flames. He waved his hands calmly, but the fire didn't go out. A savage growl born of agony and fury bellowed out of him. I tore against the spell holding me frozen, trying to free myself. I might as well have tried to move the sun for all the good it did me. I was stuck. All I could do was watch in horror.

As Nero battled against the fire consuming him, the magic holding the shifters weakened. His prisoners dropped from the wall. One of them, a young man with a shaved head and a dark goatee, lifted his gun. He didn't look like he trusted the fire to handle an angel. He was going to shoot Nero himself.

I couldn't let that happen. I continued to fight the spell holding me. There had to be a way out of this. Nero had broken the spell. How?

Stop fighting, stop pushing. Don't try to break the magic holding you, Nero's voice said in my head. *Let yourself fall through the spell.*

Any other time, I might have questioned the voice—and my sanity—but I was out of options and had no time to question anything. So I listened. I stopped fighting. I let go and let myself fall. I could feel the spell shatter all around me, its grip on me broken. I stumbled forward, quickly turning that stumble into a single-minded dash toward Nero. I had to help him.

I didn't know how I was going to put out the fire on him. I had this odd feeling that if I could just touch him, everything would be fine. I jumped at him, throwing my arms around him. A gun went off, but the bullet sliced past us. And the moment Nero and I collided, the flames died. He stepped back, catching our fall before we hit the floor.

"Are you all right?" I asked, lifting my hand to his cheek. The skin was red and hot to the touch, but the fire hadn't scorched him like it should have. He must have used magic to protect his body from the heat.

"Fine." He glanced down at his arms. The flames had burned off his shirt sleeves to the elbows, and the exposed skin was freckled with blisters. Apparently, his magic hadn't protected him completely. If that fire had gone on any longer, it might have actually killed him.

"How did you do that?" Carver demanded, his dark eyes glaring at me. "You shouldn't have been able to do that!"

I didn't have a clue how I'd put out the fire on Nero, but I wasn't going to tell the witch that. I smirked at him instead.

"Another failed spell, witch?" the pack leader said.

"What does it take to kill them?" commented the woman beside her.

"A bullet in the head," the goatee guy said, lifting his gun to shoot at us again.

Nero's eyes flashed gold, then melted to silver. He lifted his hand, flicking the shifter's gun away with a crack of psychic magic. A second blast glued them all to the wall again.

"Let's try this again," Nero said, striding up to them, every step dripping with pure menace. "What are you doing on this ship?"

"Screw you," Mr. Goatee spat out.

A psychic wave shot out of Nero, slamming the shifter's head against the wall. Nero watched him cooly, even as blood dribbled down the wall in crimson streams.

"You," Nero said, his head snapping around to Carver. "You are a witch in a band of shifters. Why are you working with them?"

The witch laughed with the kind of desperate glee that bordered on madness. "What makes you think they're not working for me?"

"Your days of commanding others are long gone," Nero said, his eyes merciless. "Now answer my question."

Carver's eyes danced between Nero and the shifters. "I want immunity. I know what the Legion does to its prisoners. If I tell you what you want to know, I go free. You don't kill me, and I don't end up a permanent resident in the Legion's prison."

"Very well."

"On your honor as an angel."

"On my honor as an angel, if you tell me what I need to know, I won't kill you or take you prisoner."

Carver's eyes flickered to me. "And you won't order her to do it either. Or any other member of the Legion. Or anyone outside the Legion acting on your orders."

"Are you finished?" Nero looked almost amused, which Carver should have known was a bad sign in an angel.

Instead, he appeared relieved. "Yes."

"All right. Now that you've miraculously evaded death's door, tell me what you and your furry companions have been up to."

"They hired me to—"

"Pyralis, you tell them, and I'll kill you!" the pack leader snarled.

"Sorry, Luna," he said. "I'm more afraid of him than I am of you."

"Only fools join the Legion of Angels, and only fools make deals with them," said Mr. Goatee.

"Silence."

Nero's voice snapped, and for a brief moment, it was like all the air had been sucked out of the room. The shifters opened their mouths to speak, but no sound came out. Hey, that was a neat trick—and very disturbing. The shifters were shouting their heads off, and I couldn't hear a single word.

Gods, I sure was glad Nero had never performed that spell on me.

"Not you," Nero said to a gaping Carver. "You need to talk. Now."

"Luna came to me a couple of weeks ago, right after the Legion put an end to the demons' army recruitment in New York," the witch spoke quickly. "The Legion inquisitors' investigation has hit the city's supernaturals hard, but especially vampires, witches, and shifters."

We'd found those three supernatural groups had been infiltrated, so it made sense Nyx's people were concentrating on weeding out the defectors in their midst.

"Among the shifters, Luna's pack was hit the hardest. Five of her own turned, and she didn't even notice." Carver looked at Luna, who was shouting soundlessly, her voice still held captive by Nero's spell. "So she decided to take the heat off of the shifters."

"By putting the heat onto someone else," I realized. "She set up the witches. That's why she came to you. Only a witch could use those powerful potions. Luna needed you to make it look like the witch covens were killing all those people."

"Yes," said Carver.

"I was at the shifter club earlier today. You almost killed your own people," I said to Luna, the bitter taste of disgust coating my tongue. "You *did* kill nearly a hundred vampires. And for what? Because you were too weak to keep control of your own people—and to deal with what they did."

With her mouth out of order, she resorted to flipping me off.

"She believed an attack on the shifters would draw suspicion away from the shifter community," said Carver. "And she had attacks planned against all supernaturals in the city except the witches themselves. The Legion would have eventually taken the witches into custody."

And the inquisitors wouldn't have listened to their pleas of innocence either. When the witches didn't break under torture, Nyx's team would have decided the demons' spell prevented them from confessing, just like the other witches. Luna had worked everything out. Well, almost everything.

"Your mistake was to attack the Legion," Nero told her.

"She assumed if you were attacked, you would immediately take the coven leaders into custody," said Carver.

"You should never venture to make assumptions about the Legion of Angels. Well, except that if you misbehave, we will catch you." He shot them a hard smile. "You can *always* assume that."

Carver cringed.

"The Legion found evidence of a fight between vampires and witches in some tunnels outside the city. The same poison used in the Brick Palace was found there. What was that about?" I asked him.

"That is where Luna had me test the poison to prove it worked."

"You're all sick."

"The world is sick," Carver told me. "Surely, the Legion has taught you that."

I frowned. "If you want to frame the witches by attacking all of the other supernaturals, then why are you trying to kill the witches here?"

"This isn't an attack. It's a retreat," said Nero. "They're here to steal the ship. You are the thief." He looked at Carver. "You've been stealing poisons and explosives from the witches. As a former coven leader, you know your way around the university—and around their wards. But you're not as clever as you think you are. The witches caught you in the act tonight, and you fled. When we took chase, you realized the game was over."

"You shouldn't have been able to track me here," said Carver. "I took precautions."

"You accounted for our magic and our technology, but not for the human element," Nero said, glancing at me.

"How did you find me?" he asked.

"New York is a busy city," I told him. "There are people everywhere, and a ninja is kind of hard to miss."

"You bribed them." Carver laughed. It was a sad, defeated laugh. "I never would have expected that from the Legion. You consider yourselves so holy, too dignified for such base things."

"I'm neither holy nor dignified."

Carver looked at me for a few seconds, then he said to Nero, "She is the most dangerous weapon the Legion of Angels has."

I was about to dispute the accusation, but Nero spoke first. "Yes. She is."

What the hell was that supposed to mean?

"You aided the shifters in their attacks on a hundred and fifty people," Nero said to the witch. "You poisoned vampires, tried to poison shifters, and tried to blow up Legion soldiers—twice. You stole highly dangerous materials from the witch coven leaders of New York in an attempt to frame them. In doing all of this, you impeded a vital Legion investigation. Demons are no laughing matter. The last time they gained a foothold into our world, the Earth was nearly torn apart. You might not have helped them directly, but you prevented us from catching the people who did. And all because of your childish need to enact revenge against the witches who removed you from power." Nero's words dripped icicles. "The Legion of Angels are the protectors who stand between monsters and civilization, between hell and Earth. You have not simply betrayed us. You have betrayed all of humanity."

"You promised not to kill me if I told you what you want to know," Carver spluttered nervously, his hands quaking against the invisible bonds holding him to the wall.

"Yes, I did."

"You also promised not to torture me."

"Indeed." Nero's smile was almost feral.

"And you said you wouldn't order anyone to kill me."

"I don't have to." Nero waved his hand, and Luna fell off the wall. "She already promised you she would kill you, and she isn't the sort of person to make empty threats."

Luna advanced toward Carver, gold flashing in her eyes as she drew a knife.

"You can't kill me!" he squealed. "That's what he wants."

"I don't care what he wants. I made a promise to you, and I'm going to fulfill it." She flipped the knife around in her hand.

"He'll just kill you afterwards."

Her mouth pulled back into a snarl. "But you'll die first."

Carver shook and thrashed against the psychic spell Nero had cast to hold him in place, but he didn't have the magic to overpower an angel. He wasn't moving an inch unless Nero allowed it.

"Wait!" Carver shouted, his terrified gaze darting to Nero. "If they couldn't get away, they were going to blow this boat out of the sky. There are bombs all over the ship."

"Where are these bombs?" Nero asked.

"Here," Luna said with a demented smile. Her hand darted to a button on her wrist band.

The wall behind her exploded, taking her and the rest of her pack with it. The blast shot me and Nero across the room. His body closed around mine, shielding me from the force of the explosion—and from the impact as we slammed hard into a metal beam. I got to my feet, my body groaning in wretched protest. I looked back at Nero, who was shaking his head like it wasn't on right.

"Are you ok?" I asked him.

"Fine," his voice ground out. Gods, he sounded even worse than I felt. Of course he did. He'd been soaked in poison twice, set on fire by magic flames, then nearly ripped apart by an explosion.

A rush of movement caught my eye. Carver was running for the big, gaping hole the explosion had blown in the side of the ship. Luna must have miscalculated when she'd blown up herself and her pack. She must have thought she'd take Carver and us with them. Carver was taking full advantage of her mistake.

Nero waved his hand at the witch. Nothing happened. Frowning, he grabbed one of his knives and hurled it at Carver, but the witch was already on his way out. I ran to the hole, staring down as a parachute ballooned up. He'd come prepared. Nero drew another knife, aiming it for the parachute. Before he could throw it, however, a second explosion went off, blasting us out of the airship.

CHAPTER 21

STEAM WITCH

*N*ero's hand locked around mine, snapping us both back into the airship. As our feet hit the floor, his wings folded in, then faded away in a puff of golden smoke. But our problems weren't over. A wall of flames raged in front of us, crackling and swaying in the wind blowing inside from the big hole at our backs. Nero waved his hand, but just like last time, nothing happened.

"This is aggravating," he said.

"Never had performance issues before?" I quipped, smirking as I pulled a fire extinguisher off the wall.

He gave me an inscrutable look. "You live dangerously."

"Because I'm teasing an angel?"

"Among many things."

It took the entire contents of the fire extinguisher to put out the flames, so I hoped there weren't any more fires. I wasn't counting on luck, though. Another explosion rocked the ship. It sounded like it had come from the other end. Just how many bombs had the shifters hidden? So this was their contingency plan. They were going to blow us up along with them so no one ever knew what they'd done, so that the

Legion wouldn't punish the entire shifter community for their crimes. If Luna and her pack weren't so murder-crazy, I might have admired their self-sacrificing bravery.

"We have to wake up the witches," I told Nero. "And get them working on finding and disabling those bombs before any more of them go off. And we'd better move fast. We're already losing altitude."

"That wasn't an explosion," he replied. "We hit something."

We ran for the bridge, where we found the pilot dead against the wall. Nero sat down at the controls, trying to coax the ship away from the building we'd hit. I ran into the party room. There, the sleeping witches were slowly blinking back into consciousness.

"We're with the Legion of Angels," I said. "A group of saboteurs has hidden bombs throughout the ship. Are any of you a Steam Witch?"

Ten people stepped forward. I'd hoped for more, but I'd have to make do with what I had. I waved at the woman in front, the one wearing a dress that looked like lingerie. Even in that outfit, she had an air of competence about her. "Come with me. I need the rest of you to search the ship for bombs and disarm them."

Then I turned and walked back to the bridge, the lingerie engineer following close on my heels. Nero didn't look up from the controls when we entered the room.

"We're still dropping," he said.

The engineer hurried over to a display on the wall. "We're leaking gas. One of the tanks was damaged."

"Then fix it," I said.

"It's not that easy."

"Let me make it easy for you. If we can't get this ship back up, we're going to crash and die. So I need you to fix that tank no matter what it takes," I said, shoving a tool box into her arms.

Tension melted off the witch's shoulders, her stance relaxing. "Of course," she said with perfect obedience, then turned around and walked out of the room.

"How did you do that?" Nero asked as I sat down beside him.

"I have a scary smile. I was channeling you." My head was pounding with the beginnings of one monster-sized headache.

"Your eyes are glowing."

"Are they? Weird."

He gave me a strange look.

"Forget my eyes," I said, looking out of the front window. "Worry about that!"

We were headed straight for a wall of skyscrapers, and with the airship sinking by the minute, we couldn't get over them.

"I see it. I'm turning the ship to go around it," he replied with perfect calmness.

"The ship doesn't feel like it's turning," I said, my voice anything but calm.

"It turns slowly."

Any normal person would have closed their eyes tightly and waited for this to all be over, but I'd given up the luxury of normalcy the day I'd traded in my old life to join the Legion. I had to be brave and strong and smart, even if I didn't feel like any of those things right now. Right now, staring at the skyscraper growing bigger and bigger in the window, I feared it was the last thing I'd ever see. Maybe it was that fear that compelled me to do what I did next—or maybe it was just an acknowledgement of how short life was. Whatever my reasons were, I took Nero's hand and squeezed it. The ship was still turning, but it wouldn't be enough. I just knew it wouldn't be. I drew in a deep breath…

As I exhaled, the airship lifted, and we slipped over the top of the buildings, missing them by mere inches. The engineer had come through! Nero's hand slid out from mine, and his fingers began flashing across the controls with inhuman speed.

"I'm taking us out of the city," he said. "There's less to hit out—"

A ragged thump pierced his words as the airship dropped, grazing the top of a building. A moment later, we rose again. That was the good news. The bad news came when I turned to look at Nero—and found him passed out on the controls.

CHAPTER 22

BATTLE OF WILLS

*W*hat could make an angel lose consciousness? I didn't know the answer, but I had a feeling it wasn't just one thing, but rather the combination of a series of events over the past hour that had chipped away at his magic and body. He wasn't looking good. His dark shirt had hidden the blood before, but it stained the beige leather seat. When I moved in for a closer look at him, I found tears in the smooth fabric—and deep lacerations and burns across his back.

I stood, squatting down into my knees. Even in sleep, Nero's face tightened with pain when I lifted him into my arms. I tried not to shake him as I moved him into a side cabin beside the bridge that looked like the captain's office. After laying him onto the sofa, I ran back into the party room.

"I need someone who knows how to pilot this ship," I announced, surprised by the calm command in my voice.

"I can do it," a man said, stepping forward. He didn't look much older than sixteen, but I wasn't in any position to be picky right now. I waved for him to follow me to the bridge.

Once there, I said, "Keep us out of the city. And make sure the ship doesn't hit anything."

Then I pulled open every cabinet in the room until I found a first aid kit. I was making a lot of noise, but my young pilot kept his eyes firmly on his job. I ran into the captain's office, carrying the kit.

I sat on the edge of the sofa. Nero was beginning to stir, but it was obviously an action born from sheer willpower alone. A quick examination revealed that he wasn't healing at all. In fact, he was getting worse. Blood was everywhere, and his previously hot skin was cool to the touch. I used a pair of scissors from the kit to cut the ruined shirt and vest from his torso. Like on his back, deep cuts crisscrossed his chest, splitting down his abdomen. I shook a bottle of healing potion, then popped the lid.

Nero's hand darted up, catching mine. "This isn't how I pictured it."

"Our mission on the ship?" I slipped free of his hold and poured the potion over his wounds.

"No, not the mission." Nero winced as pale smoke sizzled up from the cuts the potion had touched. "It's not how I pictured the first time you took off my clothes."

My cheeks warmed, despite myself. But this was no time to be self-conscious. I continued to douse his wounds with the healing potion.

He reached up, his hand cupping my cheek. "You're blushing. You look so beautiful like this." His eyes hardened as they flickered to my bleeding shoulder. "You're hurt." He dropped his hand, resting it below my wound.

"I'm fine." I peeled his hand from my arm. "Worry about yourself."

"I am an angel. I will be fine." His body didn't agree. A wet cough trailed his confident assertion, splattering his lips with blood.

Desperation shook me, and I grabbed another bottle of healing potion, spraying him again. "It's not working," I said in despair as his wounds smoked but didn't show any signs of healing. "I'm going to get a witch to heal you."

"They can't help me. The wounds are too deep," he told me.

"Can you heal yourself?"

"As you noted before, my magic is not cooperating at the moment. My body is too overtaxed from all the damage it's taken."

I grabbed the knife. "Take my blood."

"You're injured."

"I'm fine. Just do it."

He knocked the knife from my hand. "No." When I reached for it, he grabbed hold of my wrist.

"Let go, you stubborn angel!"

"No."

I pushed harder. He didn't let go, even as blood gushed from his wounds. I stopped moving. I was only making things worse.

"Why won't you let me heal you?" I demanded.

"You're hurt. You need your strength, not for me to take it. I would have to take so much blood, it could kill you."

"I'll stop you before then."

"Do you really think you are strong enough to fight me when the hunger takes over? When the brakes are off?"

"I can take you."

"No, you can't. You're not ready to face me when I'm in that state." He let out a hard, tortured laugh. "I want nothing more than to drink from you, Leda, to take what you're offering." He traced his finger down my throat. "Your blood is as sweet as the Nectar of the gods, and I've been craving it since the moment I first tasted you."

My pulse throbbed against his finger, begging him to take the plunge.

"But I can't." He dropped his hand from my throat. "I would drain you dry, and there's nothing either of us could do to stop me."

"You are a phenomenally stubborn man. I'm sure you can control yourself," I said.

"No, I couldn't. Your blood is my trigger, Leda. Something about it dissolves my willpower."

"I have enough willpower for the both of us."

His chest buzzed with a low, deep laugh. "It doesn't work that way."

"You stupid, stubborn angel." I didn't fight him. I couldn't risk hurting him any more than I already had. "Just let me heal you."

"No."

But I wasn't giving up. I refused to let him die. I moved quickly, my fangs flashing out to bite down on my wrist. As blood bubbled up to the surface, I pushed my hand into his face. Silver flashed in his eyes, but he didn't make a move toward me.

"I thought my blood made you lose control," I all but growled in frustration. What did it take for him to let me heal him?

"It does," he said, his face strained, his eyes following the drop of blood as it slid across my wrist.

I could tell he was barely holding himself together. He was about to crack. Nero Windstriker, the angel of New York, the man whose life was defined by his absolute willpower, was breaking down because of me. It would have been sexy if he weren't dying right in front of me. I could feel his blood flowing out of his body, and it sang to me like nothing ever had. I clenched my teeth and ignored its call. He did not need me to drink from him right now. He was weak enough already.

Nero looked away from the blood trickling down my wrist, his eyes meeting mine. "If you don't stop hurting your-self, I *will* knock you unconscious."

"Why are you doing this?" I growled at him.

"I'm protecting you. If something happened to you, I…" He shook his head.

"You'd have to find someone else to torture?"

"There is no one else."

"There's a whole Legion full of them ripe for torture. I'm sure you could find a few."

He wrapped the arm of his torn shirt around my wrist. "There's no one like you," he said quietly, his eyes serious. And I didn't think he was talking about torturing me with his training sessions anymore. He lifted my hand to his lips, kissing my fingers.

Another collision rocked the ship. The floor lurched, and books flew across the room—along with all the furniture in the cabin. Nero's arms closed around me, shielding my body, but his grip slipped when we hit something else, throwing him against the wall. I peeled my aching body off the ground as the new pilot burst through the door.

"I thought I told you not to hit anything," I growled.

"The explosions earlier damaged everything. The ship is falling apart. We've lost the ability to steer," he said, fear jumbling all his words together. "We're coming up on the wall, and I can't turn us away. We're going to hit it."

CHAPTER 23

"*W*hat do we do?" the pilot asked, his voice cracking with panic.

I didn't have a clue. I looked across the room, trying to find Nero. And I found him—unconscious on the floor. The pilot was looking at me with hopeful desperation, like I had the answers to all of our problems. Nero would have known what to do, but I just…didn't.

"How long do we have?" I asked him.

"Five minutes at the most."

"Find the engineer. Bring her to the bridge," I said.

Apparently assured that I knew what I was doing, the pilot nodded, then ran back into the corridor. I glanced down at Nero. He was so pale now. I wasn't sure he'd survive.

"I know you won't like this," I said, lowering beside him. "But I'm not giving you a choice."

Setting his head on my lap, I pushed my bleeding wrist against his mouth. His nose twitched, and he inhaled the scent of my blood. Like magic, his hands jerked up, closing around my fingers, pushing my wrist to his mouth. When his fangs broke the skin, fire flashed through my veins. The long, powerful draws of his mouth fed that fire, pushing it higher until the feverish bliss consumed my entire body.

Nero drank deeply from me. Soon, dizzying waves spilled across me, drowning me in a dark and dangerous ecstasy that part of me knew would kill me. Nero must have known it too, but he didn't stop. He couldn't stop, I realized. His eyelids flickered rapidly, as though he were still caught inside of a dream.

"Nero," I said, trying to free my wrist.

His grip tightened around my hand, his fingers digging in deeper. He wasn't letting go without a fight, and I wasn't strong enough to beat him in a fair one. Purple and black and pink dots danced in front of my eyes. Blinking back the impending darkness, I grabbed the handle of the healing kit I'd brought along. I swung hard, knocking him over the head. His body went limp. I disengaged my wrist from his mouth, slid him off of me, and got shakily to my feet.

I ran back to the bridge, bumping against the walls a few times along the way. My head still spinning, I stumbled into the co-pilot seat. Sitting proved to be easier than standing, though I certainly was in no shape to drive anything, especially a damaged airship. I pulled at the steering wheel anyway, just in case I could will it to work again. It didn't cooperate.

The pilot rushed onto the bridge, the engineer right beside him. Both of them looked sure they were going to die. Granted, the situation was dire, but I wasn't giving up so easily. If we hit the great wall, the impact would either destroy us or a part of the wall—or both. And if the wall broke, that would open the way for the monsters and the other nasties who lived on the Black Plains to invade the Earth's remaining civilized lands. More than just the people on this ship were going to die if we didn't get a handle on the situation.

"We're descending again," I told the engineer.

"The ship is too damaged. I can't keep us up in the air. Sooner or later, we're going to crash."

"Can you make it later?"

"What?"

"I need you to bring us over the wall."

"But then we'll crash on the Wilds side," she said in horror.

"Yes, we'll crash in the Black Plains, but that's better than crashing into the wall."

She shook her head. "I can't do it. The gas tanks are ruined. There isn't enough left to lift us up that high."

"Are you a Steam Witch or not?" I demanded. "If you don't have enough gas, then enchant the hell out of what you do have. Put some more magic into it, and get us over that wall."

That weird dazed look slid over her eyes. She nodded and ran back down the hall—I hoped to the engine room. The wall was…well, close. There wasn't really another word for it. Except maybe big. And thick. And alight with a golden glow. Ok, that was more than one word. I squinted out of the front window. Glowing? It shouldn't be glowing. That meant someone had turned the magic on, and that if we hit it, we'd disintegrate into a fiery plume long before we could damage the wall. There were no paranormal soldiers posted here, but someone must have seen us coming and flipped on the wall's power.

Slowly, the airship began to rise. We might just survive this yet. But my moment of hope was cut short when the ship shook and dropped. My head slammed against the controls. My splotchy vision faded to darkness, and I finally lost my futile battle with consciousness.

———

I BLINKED AWAKE A FEW SECONDS LATER. AT LEAST IT HAD to be just a few seconds later because the wall was still looming in front of us. It took me longer than it should have to realize we weren't moving any closer to it. We were just stuck in time.

I rose from my chair, clenching my jaw through the fresh dose of pain rushing to my head. Holding tightly to the seat back, I stepped closer to the window and looked down at the ground.

A woman in leather armor stood in front of the wall, her hands lifted in the air, her long black hair whipping in the wind. Nyx, the First Angel. Her white wings were spread wide. The glow of the golden magic that pulsed out from the wall hit them, lighting up the gold flecks in her feathers. They looked like they were sparkling with millions of tiny glitter particles. Slowly, she lowered her hands, and the airship dipped with them, coasting toward the ground. She was holding up a whole ship with her psychic power alone. The magic Nyx could wield was simply mind-boggling.

Darkness flickered in front of my eyes, threatening to draw me back under the blanket of unconsciousness. I gripped the chair harder and tried to stay awake. Gods, I was tired. Was I even awake? Maybe I was dreaming—or dead.

It felt real enough when the ship touched down on the ground. I took another step toward the window to get a closer look, but my legs collapsed out from under me. Someone caught my fall. I turned slowly around, expecting to find the pilot. Instead, I found Nero.

"You should still be sleeping," I said groggily.

He swept me off my feet, holding me protectively to him. Well, I was going to call it protective at least. That sounded better than 'reprimanding' or 'furious'. I set my head on his bare shoulder, happy in my little delusion.

"You foolish woman," he said as he carried me into the captain's office. "What did you do to yourself?"

"Healed you with my blood." Everything was spinning all around me, so I closed my eyes. I felt him lower me onto the sofa.

"It was more of a rhetorical question." He sighed. "I specifically ordered you not to give me your blood."

"And I specifically didn't listen." I opened my eyes and shot him a saucy grin. "Because you were being pigheaded."

"That is rich coming from you."

"I'm not pigheaded. I'm just strong-willed. I'm sure you appreciate the difference."

He traced his hand down my arm, his touch feather-soft. "What am I going to do with you?"

"You could try thanking me for saving your life." I shivered as a warm tingle melted into my skin, burning hotter the deeper it penetrated. A feverish sweat broke out all across my body. "Stop that," I hissed at him. "Turn off that…whatever magic you're using on me. You can't take advantage of me while I'm too weak to stop you."

Nero chuckled. "I'm trying to heal you, not seduce you. Now be quiet and let me concentrate."

I sealed my lips and waited, trying not to think about how good his magic felt. Or about how much that feeling reminded me of drinking from him, of the way his blood had pulsed through me. I coughed, swallowing the moan humming inside my throat.

"All finished," he said after what felt like an eternity of agonizing ecstasy.

I very nearly cried when he withdrew his hand from my arm. He'd healed my wounds, but as the last echoes of his magic left me, I felt even worse than before. I felt empty. Like a hollow shell.

"Wait," I said, taking hold of his hand before I could think better of it.

Nero waited, his face unreadable.

"I…" I cleared my throat. "I'm glad you didn't die."

"Your blood healed me, but giving it to me nearly killed you. You are reckless. And foolish."

My heart plunging in my chest, I drew my hand away, but he caught it. His fingers spread, intertwining with mine as he dipped his head to mine.

"I'm glad you didn't die too," he whispered against my lips.

Then, his mouth swooped down on mine. He kissed me with a hunger that shattered his marble facade, leaving only the savagely sensual beast within, the part of him that I'd caught only a taste of before. I grasped at his naked back, pulling him closer with a desperate desire that was as dark as his own.

Suddenly, Nero froze. He pulled away, jumping up to his feet. I jumped up after him, more than ready to pull him back down with me. Until I saw her. Nyx was standing in the doorway, one hand leaning casually against the frame, the other propped up on her hip.

"Don't let me stop you from this joyful celebration of your triumph over death," she said, amusement shining in her icy blue eyes.

Nero stood beside me, as still as a statue. The inevitable wave of self-consciousness hit me, and I took a step away from him. Though my body was perfectly alert—*overly* alert even—my head was still a bit foggy. I miscalculated, and my shoulder brushed against the wall.

"Take a few minutes to rest," Nyx said. "You two just saved the hundred people aboard this airship from being blown to bits."

"Just doing our job," I told her.

Her dark red lips lifted into a smile. "Yes, you really did."

CHAPTER 24

LIFE AND DEATH

*A*fter a few minutes, my head cleared enough for me to try walking again. I made it down the corridor—all the way to the big hole in the ship at the end—without tripping or bumping into anything. Nero closed up beside me. I hadn't seen him since he'd left the captain's office with Nyx earlier.

Outside the airship, the Legion was there in full force, loading the witches into the Legion vans so they could be taken back to the city for proper care. The soldiers gave me and Nero curious looks as we passed them on our way to Nyx. The First Angel was directing the whole scene with natural grace, like she'd been made for nothing else. She was the most powerful angel on Earth. She commanded armies and wielded great magic. She could save crashing airships and read our minds from hundreds of miles away. That must have been how she ended up here at the right place and the right time.

"Not exactly," Nero said. "I messaged her when we came aboard the airship."

"When did you have time to do that?" I asked. "And stop reading my thoughts."

"I can multitask," he replied to my first question. "And it's hard to block you out when you want me to hear your thoughts."

"I don't ever want you to hear my thoughts."

"You're not a very good liar."

"And you're not a very good conversationalist," I shot back. "So you updated Nyx when the ship was damaged?"

"No, I learned of your troubles when pieces of New York's all-night party airship began falling out of the sky," the First Angel said, waving us closer. "When I heard the Sunken Ship was on a collision course for the wall, I came to stop it."

"You're so powerful," I told her.

"I'm the First Angel, the most powerful angel in the world, second only to the gods." She winked at me, as though she didn't take herself as seriously as she knew she should. "I've sent soldiers to bring in New York's pack leaders for questioning. If there's a demon behind this, we will find out."

"The shifters framed the witches to draw attention away from themselves in the Legion's investigation," I said. "And they convinced an embittered witch to help them."

"Yes, Colonel Windstriker filled me in on what you've discovered." Her full, red lips tightened into a hard line. "The shifters will soon realize that their efforts have produced the opposite effect as they'd hoped. They will be at the forefront of our continued investigation into the demon incursion."

I hadn't expected anything different. The Legion operated under the principle of absolute authority. They had to show everyone that they were in control—and that no one could get away with undermining that control.

"You're covered in blood and missing half of your

clothes," Nyx told us. "Get back to New York. I expect the full report on your adventure by tomorrow morning."

We bowed, then walked toward the cluster of vans parked outside the downed airship. But Nero didn't stop at the vans. He continued past them.

"What is *that*?" I said, gawking at the vehicle parked on the grass.

"A car." He opened the door for me.

"That's not a car. It's a rocket on wheels," I told him, getting in.

He walked around to the driver's side and turned the car on. "That is an apt description," he agreed as the engine roared to life. "It's the latest development in Magitech. This car can travel over twice as fast as a normal car."

"Then it's a good thing you have supernatural reflexes."

"Indeed it is."

I tapped the leather armrest. "You're not color-blind, are you?"

"No."

"Ok, so you *do* realize the outside of your car is the color of dandelions?"

"It's not my car," Nero said.

"Oh?" I took one glance out of the window, then hastily looked away. The countryside was flashing past so fast that I was feeling dizzy all over again. "Whose car is it then?"

"Nerissa's."

"Nerissa Harding, the lead scientist of the Legion's New York labs?"

"Are you surprised?"

"Actually, come to think of it, no. This gaudy thing is just her style. Totally unfiltered."

"Yes," he agreed.

"So why are we taking Nerissa's car?"

"Because it's the fastest way to get us back to the Legion. Our healers need to have a look at your injuries."

"You already healed me."

"I did not have enough magic in me to heal you completely."

"I can handle a few bruises," I told him.

"I know you can." He glanced over at me, which, considering the speed the car was moving at, was downright reckless. His eyes flickered back to the road.

"This isn't about my injuries. You want to talk to me," I realized.

"Yes."

I squeezed my hands together. "Oh, well, ok."

For someone so eager to talk to me, he sure wasn't very talkative. We passed the rest of the drive in silence. That silence stretched on as we parked under the Legion's New York building, and it held as we walked down the hall to his office. It was only after he closed the door behind us that Nero spoke.

"Please sit down," he said, taking the seat behind his desk.

"Am I in trouble?" I asked as I sat down opposite him.

He folded his hands together on the tabletop. "Do you remember what I said to you all when you joined the Legion?"

He'd said a lot of things.

"About obedience," Nero continued.

"Ah, so that was a *yes* to being in trouble." I cleared my throat. "You told us that when we're in a crisis, you need to know we will follow your commands without question."

"Your memory far exceeds your execution. You did not follow my commands tonight."

I didn't say anything. What was there to say? He was completely right.

"You gave me your blood even when I told you not to. You put yourself at risk." I opened my mouth to speak, but he cut in. "I'm not finished. You were reckless and disobedient. I should punish you for it."

"But you're not going to?" I said, shooting him a hopeful smile. "Because I saved your life."

"This is the second time you disobeyed me directly. And I can't even count the number of times you've done something you knew I wouldn't approve of." He tapped his fingers across his desk. "Last month, you disobeyed me and went after me on the Black Plains. Why?"

"Because you're obviously incapable of taking care of yourself," I teased.

"No jokes. Tell me why you did it."

"Because it was the right thing to do," I said.

"Perhaps, but it wasn't the right thing for you to do as a soldier of the Legion. I need my soldiers to obey me, and time and time again, you refuse. You know you need to follow the rules to survive the Legion, to receive more of the gods' gifts of magic, gifts you need to save your brother. This is essential. And yet you still disobey me. Why?"

"Zane wouldn't want me to turn off my compassion to save him. He wouldn't want me to stop being who I am. When I see my brother again, I want to be able to look him in the eye and not hate what I've become."

Nero was quiet for a few moments, then he said, "You are a good person."

"Thank you."

"But you are a lousy soldier," he added. "How am I supposed to help you when you don't even listen to what I say? How will I get you to the ninth level?"

He seemed to be talking to himself, but I answered anyway. "I guess you have your work cut out for you."

"Yes." He frowned.

"Nyx wants me to be an angel," I added.

"How do you know?"

"I heard you talking to her."

"That conversation wasn't for your ears."

"Embarrassed?"

"No, I have not hidden anything from you, Leda. You know how I feel."

"You want to sleep with me."

"That is what I *want*. It's not how I *feel*."

"Is there a difference for you?" I asked.

"Yes, a big one. There's something between us, Leda. It's not just raw attraction. That is merely a consequence of our connection."

"So you do have feelings," I said, smiling. "Amazing. I thought angels were immune."

"Not immune. Not at all. Just as our senses are stronger, so are our feelings. We feel more—deeper—than others. Which is why we must control our feelings."

"Well, when I'm an angel, I'm going to feel everything." I smirked at him.

"Yes, I think you will. You will tear the heavens asunder." He set his hand on my cheek. "And I'm helping you on that catastrophic path." He shook his head slowly, as though he couldn't believe what he was doing.

"Nyx wants you to help me," I told him.

"Nyx is…an unusual angel. She feels too."

"So the Legion didn't squeeze that out of her."

"She didn't work her way up the ranks."

I looked at him in confusion.

"Nyx wasn't made an angel. She was born one," he explained.

"I didn't know that could happen."

"She is the only demigod ever born."

And that explained a lot about Nyx—and her complex, often contradictory personality. She was of two worlds, of heaven and Earth.

"But I didn't want to talk about her," Nero said, standing.

"You wanted to talk about my punishment."

"I will have to punish you. There is no way around it. I cannot allow everyone else to think they can disobey me."

I offered him a small smile. "Pushups?"

"I think we are beyond that, Leda."

"I know," I sighed. "So what will it be?"

"You will clean the Legion's common area toilets once a day for a week."

"That's not a very supernatural punishment," I pointed out.

"Sometimes the simple ones are the best."

"Or the worst." I crinkled up my nose. I could almost smell the public toilets from here. "I'd rather take the pushups. Or how about I fight those hell dogs every day for a week?"

"You don't get a choice in your punishment. That defeats the purpose. Punishments aren't meant to be pleasant."

"Then I guess I'll just have to hope the toilets don't fight back."

He gave me a strange look. "I don't want to hurt you, you know."

"I know." I set my hand on his. "Vile as the toilets may be, they won't kill me. If you really wanted to hurt me, you would have assigned me extra training."

"You will be receiving that as well. Starting tomorrow, you can look forward to getting up half an hour earlier."

"So much for not wanting to hurt me," I muttered.

"That is not a punishment. I want you to train more because I know you can do better if I just push you hard enough." He intertwined his fingers with mine. "Even though it hurts me. Every punch. Every time I hit you when we're training."

"Maybe you need to learn to punch better," I teased him.

"Not that sort of pain, Leda."

I looked into his eyes and saw something unexpected. "You have feelings for me. Like *real* feelings."

"Yes."

"But that's so…human of you."

"I know," he said. "I can't afford to be human. To feel. To doubt. To be irrational… On the airship, when you lost consciousness, I had to go to you. I had to heal you, even though I was not fully healed myself. I needed every bit of magic in me to be an effective soldier, and I gave some of it to you. It was a decision devoid of reason."

"Feelings have no reason, no logic. They just are," I said.

"My behavior was unbefitting of a soldier of the Legion."

Amusement tickled my lips. "Maybe you'll have to punish yourself too."

"Yes," he agreed seriously.

"Pushups?" I struggled to keep a straight face.

"Not harsh enough."

"How about if I sit on you while you do them?"

Laughter burst from his mouth, beautiful, unchecked. I loved to hear him laugh. Something about it filled me with silly, sappy happiness.

"I feel the same, Nero. About you," I told him.

He watched me, saying nothing.

"I'm not rational when you're hurt either," I continued.

"Even so, I cannot excuse your disobedience, no matter how good your intentions were. I can't let you off the hook."

"I know," I sighed.

"The angel in me cannot allow it, even though your words make the man in me dare to hope."

"Hope about what?"

His voice dipped lower. "Hope that you will be amenable to my proposition."

"I don't think I'm ready for any propositions, Nero. I'm too deep in this already."

"Deep in what?"

"In you," I told him.

A smile twisted his lips. "I wasn't talking about *that* kind of proposition."

"What other kind could you mean?"

"I just want to ask you to dinner."

There was no such thing as 'just dinner' for us. Warning sirens blared inside of my head. If anything, his proposition was more dangerous than the other—because it came with feelings attached. His eyes burned with intentions unspoken but not unfathomable. I knew his endgame. He didn't just want to seduce me; he wanted to make me fall for him through and through, heart and soul. That didn't scare me nearly as much as my eagerness to jump into the fire after him.

"I accept," I said. Wasn't facing your fears the best way to get rid of them? "But we have to go somewhere public, not to your apartment."

"You don't like my apartment?"

"It's lovely, but I think we both know what will happen if we have dinner there." In fact, I was having lurid memories of this office right now. It was making it hard to focus.

"As you wish." He kissed my hand. "I will take you some-place nice."

"And will this date happen before or after my punishment?

"I'll let you pick."

I laughed. That angel sure had a crazy sense of humor. And the crazier thing was I couldn't wait for our date. Or was it really so crazy? We worked together, fought together, had been through life and death together. What was a little dinner and dessert compared to that?

AUTHOR'S NOTE

If you want to be notified when I have a new release, head on over to my website to sign up for my mailing list at http://www.ellasummers.com/newsletter. Your e-mail address will never be shared, and you can unsubscribe at any time.

If you enjoyed *Witch's Cauldron*, I'd really appreciate if you could spread the word. One of the best ways of doing that is by leaving a review wherever you purchased this book. Thank you for your invaluable support!

Siren's Song, the third book in the *Legion of Angels* series, is now available.

ABOUT THE AUTHOR

Ella Summers has been writing stories for as long as she could read; she's been coming up with tall tales even longer than that. One of her early year masterpieces was a story about a pigtailed princess and her dragon sidekick. Nowadays, she still writes fantasy. She likes books with lots of action, adventure, and romance. When she is not busy writing or spending time with her two young children, she makes the world safe by fighting robots.

Ella is the *USA Today*, *Wall Street Journal*, and International Bestselling Author of the paranormal and fantasy series *Legion of Angels*, *Dragon Born*, and *Sorcery & Science*.

www.ellasummers.com

Made in the USA
Coppell, TX
10 January 2020